Chapter 1

"That is the stupidest idea I've ever heard." Julie sipped at her coffee and glared at her best friend.

"No, it isn't," Mary insisted. She took her own sip of coffee before leaning forward and giving Julie a scrutinizing look. "You're thirty years old and you've spent your entire life practically locked up in this ridiculous mansion. Your father is dead, there's nothing stopping you from living your life now."

Julie winced and stared morosely at the gleaming table top. "Don't soften the blow or anything, Mary."

Mary took her hand and squeezed it. "Listen, I get that your father had you convinced that you were worthless but the bastard has been dead for six months. How long are you going to continue to live in his shadow? You have no family. I'm your only friend, and that's just because I refused to let your father intimidate me, and you spend all of your time sitting on your ass in front of the television. That's no kind of life, Julie."

Julie sighed and rubbed at her forehead. Mary was right. She was wasting her life, had been for the last thirty years, but she had no idea how to start fresh. Some days just trying to leave the house felt like too much. She had been bullied and manipulated by her father for her entire life and even though he was dead, she could still hear his voice whispering in her ear. She would never be pretty enough or smart enough for him and after years of emotional torment, it was too easy to believe that what he had told her repeatedly over the years was true.

"Fine. You're right – I need to get out more. But I hardly think what you're suggesting is the right way to meet someone," she replied.

"This isn't about meeting someone," Mary answered. "This is about getting your pesky virginity out of the way so that you can relax about it, gain some self-confidence, and *then* meet someone."

"And you think that paying someone to rid me of my pesky v-card is going to boost my self-confidence?" Julie asked with exasperation. "I hate to tell you this, Mare, but having sex with someone who's paid to tell me I'm beautiful isn't exactly a confidence booster."

Mary shook her head impatiently. "That isn't what I meant. You think being a virgin at thirty makes you some kind of freak and, truthfully, it does just a little."

"You're doing a bang-up job of making me feel better," Julie said sullenly.

"I'm just being honest. The truth is – you'll be hard pressed to find a guy who doesn't think it's weird that you're still a virgin at thirty. That isn't going to help your self-confidence or improve your non-existent dating skills. You need to get rid of your v-card first and this is the perfect solution. Then you can start looking for Mr. Right who will love you for who you are, not because he's being paid to."

"Hiring some – some gigolo to take my virginity is not the perfect solution! Only dirty old men hire prostitutes to have sex!" Julie replied vehemently.

"You're totally looking at it the wrong way. One, they're not called gigolo's anymore, they're called escorts, and two – "

"Fine! So I'm going to hire an escort for a night of wham bam thank-you ma'am just so I can increase my chances of finding a nice guy?" Julie sputtered. "Seriously, Mary I love you but – "

"And two," Mary drowned out Julie's protests, "it's not a wham bam scenario. These guys are professionals. They wine and dine and will do whatever it is you want them to. You don't even have to have sex with them the first time if you don't want to. You could go on a few dates and get to know them before you sleep with them."

"Yeah, for a cost!" Julie snorted.

Mary rolled her eyes. "Like you can't friggin' afford it, Daddy Warbucks. Your father did the only nice thing he ever did for you in his entire life by leaving his fortune to you. You'll never spend all of it in a lifetime, so don't even try and tell me a few thousand bucks on an escort is going to break you."

"A few thousand?" Julie's eyes widened. "Just how good are they at sex for it to cost thousands?"

Mary laughed. "They're excellent, Julie. Trust me."

Julie gave her a suspicious look. "Have you hired an escort before?"

"No. But do you remember a couple of years ago when I was hanging out with that chick, Devon?"

Julie nodded. "I remember. That girl was a freak."

"She wasn't a freak," Mary said impatiently. "Anyway, she had an important work function that she needed a date for. She hired an escort and he was perfect."

"Did she sleep with him?"

"Well, she wasn't planning on it but the guy was so goddamn charming that she ponied up the extra cash and had the best sex of her life that night." Mary grinned.

Julie rubbed her forehead again. "This is ridiculous. I can't believe I'm even having this conversation with you. I am not hiring a man to deflower me so that I can get out and meet other men. Besides, even if I lose my virginity and learn some moves in the sack, men aren't going to be interested in me. Look at me."

She glanced down at her chubby body and pulled self-consciously at her yoga pants.

"I am looking at you. I know you think that you're fat and ugly, but you're not," Mary said firmly.

"You have to say that. You're my best friend."

"No, I don't," Mary snapped. "Since when have I ever said something to you just because I had to? When your eyebrows started looking like two fuzzy caterpillars were about to have sex on your face, who told you? When you got that dreadful pixie haircut that made you look like a fairy after a three-day bender, who told you?"

"Okay, okay!" Julie could feel a grin crossing her face and she sipped again at her coffee. "You're blunt and you're mean. It's what I love most about you."

"Damn straight it is," Mary said with satisfaction. She leaned back in her chair and crossed her legs before looking at Julie's body appraisingly. "You're not fat, Julie. I know your father spent a lifetime telling you that you were but you're not. You're pleasantly plump, charmingly chubby, curvy in all the right places. You get your idea of beauty from the internet and the TV because that's all you see. You never go out in the real world. Get your ass out of those yoga pants and into clothes that fit you properly and you'll look fantastic. Guys will love your body, I guarantee it."

Julie snorted before glancing at Mary's slender body. "Says the girl who wears a size four."

"So what? Who cares? You think guys will like me better because I'm a size four and you're a size sixteen? That's bullshit. Sure, there might be guys out there who prefer skinny chicks but there are plenty of men who like their women with curves. They like a little something to hold on to during the pushin'."

Mary made a rude gesture with her hips and Julie blushed hotly, a nervous giggle escaping from between her lips before she looked away.

"See! That's exactly what I'm talking about!" Mary said triumphantly. "Sex is even mentioned in front of you and you turn into a giggly thirteen-year-old girl. You need to get sex out of the way, learn some things, before you even try dating. Trust me on this, Jules."

"Mary, I – "

"Listen – you go to the escort agency, find a guy that floats your boat, and tell him the truth. Tell him you're a virgin and you're looking to lose it and gain some valuable sex tips. Easy-peasy."

"It's not easy-peasy," Julie protested again. "Besides, what if someone found out I hired a prostitute? I'd be humiliated!"

"Who's going to find out? I'm your only friend, remember? And I'm certainly not going to tell anyone. Who does that leave? Your dead father? Who cares what that son of a bitch thinks? Besides, he's too busy burning in hell to even notice your new life."

"Mary!" Julie gave her a look of shock and Mary shrugged.

"It's true and you know it, Jules."

She jumped up and headed out of the kitchen and down the hall to Julie's father's study. Julie, muttering under her breath, followed her. She entered the study and tried to ignore the immediate twinge of guilt. Her father's study had always been off-limits to her and, even now, she felt uncomfortable standing in the room.

Mary plopped down in the black leather chair behind her father's desk and turned on his laptop. Julie crossed the room and peered over her shoulder as Mary typed.

"Vanessa's Escort Agency?" Julie scoffed. "That's original. Seriously, isn't prostitution illegal? How can she even be in business?"

"I don't know how it works," Mary replied. "I mean, being an escort isn't illegal, I'm sure they just call the sex part something different. Like, maybe they refer to it as ice cream."

"Ice cream?"

"Yeah! Like there's a cost for a perfectly legal dinner with the escort and if you want *ice cream* after, there's an additional cost." Mary laughed.

She clicked the link to the website and immediately clicked on the "our escorts" link. Despite herself, Julie stared with interest at the pictures that popped up.

"Wow," Mary said appreciatively. "These guys are friggin' dreamy."

She scrolled through the pictures of men. "Ooh, I like this one. His name is Robert and he's a ski instructor."

"No way," Julie said immediately. "He'll be way too fit for me."

Mary rolled her eyes. "They've all got rock-star bodies, Jules. That's the appeal. How about this guy? He's twenty-seven, enjoys outdoor activities and is co-owner of a gym. Nice."

"Nope," Julie replied. "Definitely not."

"Oh for the love of Pete!" Mary gave her an exasperated look. "Just pick one, Jules."

"What for? I have no intention of..."

She trailed off as Mary scrolled further down.

"What? See something you like?" Mary wiggled her eyebrows at her and then followed Julie's gaze.

"Wow...he's hot." She clicked on the man's profile. "Let's see. His name is Cal. He's thirty-three and he likes walks on the beach, romantic dinners, and fine wine. Huh. A little cliché but he's gorgeous so we'll let it pass."

Julie didn't reply. She was staring mesmerized at the man on the screen in front of her. He was smiling easily into the camera and he had an air of rugged confidence about him. He had short dark hair and green eyes and a small cleft in his chin. She studied the hard angle of his jaw and the broad shoulders clothed in an expensive dark suit. He was beautiful. She couldn't even picture approaching a man that looked like him, let alone imagine herself naked in front of him.

Mary clicked a different link and the man's face disappeared. Julie felt a tug of disappointment that quickly turned to horror when she realized Mary was typing an email.

"Mary! Stop this right now!" She squeaked.

"Nope," Mary replied. She finished typing and Julie quickly read the short message.

Hello,

My name is Julie and I'm interested in hiring an escort for the evening. Please call me at the enclosed phone number.

Sincerely,
Julie Winslow

Before Julie could stop her, Mary had clicked on the send button. She gave Mary a look of fear. "What did you just do?"

Mary grinned at her. "If you don't want to speak to them, just ignore the phone call, Jules. But if you want to change your life for the better, then answer the damn call."

She stood up and kissed Julie on the cheek. "I've got to go. I'm meeting Gary for lunch at Oasis. I love you, Jules."

"I – I love you too," Julie answered. She was still stunned at what had just transpired and she followed Mary to the front door in a daze.

Mary paused on the doorstep and gave her a hug. "Take a chance, Jules. You deserve to be happy," she whispered. She kissed her on the cheek and ran down the front steps to her car parked in the driveway.

Julie watched numbly as she drove away before shutting the door and leaning heavily against it. What the hell just happened?

Chapter 2

She was sitting on the couch watching daytime television, eating a plate of raw celery and carrots and wishing that it was ice cream, when her cell phone rang. Her heart jumped in her chest and she muted the television before reaching for it. The only person who ever called her was Mary and she studied the strange number, her pulse beginning to pound. She knew without a doubt that it was the escort agency and, feeling like she was having an out-of-body experience, she pressed the answer button.

"Hello?"

"Ms. Winslow?" A woman's voice, warm and professional sounding, spoke into her ear.

"Y-yes."

"My name is Meagan. I'm calling from Vanessa's Escort Agency regarding your earlier email."

"Oh yes, hi. Um, listen there's – "

"We're so glad you called us. Now, we do like to meet our potential clients in person so is it possible for you to drop by our office?" Meagan interrupted smoothly.

"Well, I – "

"We promise we won't take up much of your time. Does tomorrow at three work for you?"

"Okay, sure," Julie replied in a soft voice. Years of living with her domineering father, of having him constantly belittle and chastise her for her choices, had turned her into a dyed-in-the-wool people pleaser. She should never have answered the damn phone.

"Great!" Meagan replied. "I'll send you the email with our address and we'll see you tomorrow at three."

She hung up before Julie could reply. Julie set her cell phone down and stared blankly at the television. She was going to an escort agency tomorrow. What did one even wear to an escort agency?

She took a deep breath and called Mary.

* * *

She stood in front of the open elevator and bit her lip indecisively. It wasn't too late. She could simply turn and walk out of the building.

Coward.

She winced at her inner voice.

Do you want to be alone forever? You may not want to admit it, but Mary was right. Part of the reason, a big part, you're afraid to meet anyone is because you're ashamed you're a virgin at thirty. Do this. Lose it to someone who's anonymous, who'll say all the right things, and make you feel pretty. They'll show you what to do and you can stop worrying about sex and all its mysteries, and start worrying about finding the right guy. Do you really want to die alone, surrounded by cats?

No, she most certainly did not. Never mind that she was allergic to cats and couldn't go near one without breaking into hives, the principal of the thought was sound. If she didn't do something, didn't change something, she really was going to die alone. Exactly as her father predicted.

She squared her shoulders, remembering the disgust in her father's voice when he had repeatedly ridiculed her for her weight and told her no man would ever find her attractive with an ass the size of hers. He might be right. Hell, she might never find a man who found her attractive or find the courage to go on a single date. She could possibly die a lonely, sad spinster despite what she was doing, but at least she wouldn't die a lonely, sad, *virgin* spinster.

"Excuse me, ma'am? Are you going to get in the elevator?"

She jumped and turned to give the man behind her an apologetic smile. "I'm sorry. Yes, I am."

She faced forward and marched into the elevator. The man joined her and she hit the button for the twenty-fourth floor with a trembling finger. The man pressed the button for seventeen and they rode in silence.

"Have a nice day." He gave her a friendly smile and she forced herself to return it, smoothing her hands anxiously over her skirt.

"Thank you. You as well."

The elevator doors closed and she was alone. She took a shaky breath and studied herself in the reflection of the elevator doors. Mary, nearly vibrating with excitement, had helped her pick out her outfit. She was wearing a dark navy skirt that stopped just below her knees, a pale pink tank top and a grey blazer. She had left the blazer unbuttoned but after a quick look at the way her muffin top was visible, she quickly buttoned the blazer.

The elevator dinged softly and the doors slid open with a quiet hum. Expecting a hallway, she jerked with surprise when they opened into a reception area. A blonde woman, her hair pulled into an elegant chignon, was sitting behind a large wooden desk. She looked up from her computer as the elevator doors opened.

"Hello! You must be Ms. Winslow." The woman came out from behind the desk as Julie stepped into the waiting area. She held out her hand and, wiping her sweaty palm on her skirt first, Julie shook it tentatively.

"Um, yes. I am."

"It's lovely to meet you. I'm Meagan. We spoke on the phone?"

"Oh right. Of course. Hi, Meagan."

"Why don't you have a seat? Vanessa is just finishing up a phone call and will be right with you. Can I get you a cup of coffee? Tea? Glass of water?"

"No, thank you." Julie nearly fell into the oversized chair Meagan was directing her towards, and clutched her purse nervously. The waiting room was sparse but tastefully decorated and she glanced around curiously as Meagan returned to her computer.

The minutes ticked by and her anxiety grew. What she was doing was madness and she couldn't go through with it. She stood.

"Excuse me, I think I – "

A door to her left opened and a tall, silver-haired woman stepped into the waiting area.

"Hello, Ms. Winslow. My name is Vanessa Michaels. Please, come into my office."

Julie glanced at Meagan. The woman gave her an encouraging smile and she smiled weakly in return before following Vanessa into her office.

"It's nice to meet you, Julie. May I call you Julie?" The woman asked as they shook hands.

"Of course. It's nice to meet you as well, Ms. Michaels."

"Call me Vanessa." She sat down behind her desk and Julie perched nervously in the leather chair in front of the desk.

Vanessa folded her hands on the desk and stared at Julie for a moment. "So, tell me a little bit about yourself, Julie."

Julie blinked at her. "Oh, well my name is Julie Winslow – I guess you already know that – and I'm um, thirty years old. My father just passed away recently."

"I'm sorry for your loss."

"Thank you. I, um, I live by myself and I uh – I'm um – I'm looking for an escort," she finished lamely. She realized with dismay that she couldn't think of a single, interesting thing to say about herself but the woman was still staring at her silently, waiting for more.

"I – I like to read," she said desperately. She was struck with sudden inspiration. "And knit! I'm very fond of knitting."

Vanessa smiled at her. "I myself, never learned to knit. I always wanted to but I'm afraid I'm rather hopeless at crafty things."

She opened a file folder that was sitting on her desk. "Are you looking for an escort for a particular event? A wedding, perhaps? Or maybe a high school reunion?"

Julie shook her head. "No. I just wanted a date. A regular, um, date."

She wondered if that made her look even more pathetic and desperate but Vanessa just nodded.

"Very good. I assume you've seen our website. Was there someone in particular that caught your interest?"

Julie wiped her hands down her skirt again. "Yes. I think his name was Cal?"

Vanessa nodded. "Excellent choice."

She pushed some papers across her desk. "There is a bit of paperwork to go over. We do a background check, of course, on all of our clients. The safety of our employees is our utmost concern. If you pass the background check, we will email you information about the escort of your choice. All of our escorts are personally recruited by myself and extensive personal background and criminal checks are completed on them before they're hired to work for my company. You don't have to worry about mental illnesses, sexually transmitted diseases, or anything of that sort. You'll see all of their medical history and the information from the background check in the documentation we email you."

She turned the page on the stack of papers in front of her. "We also ask that you sign a confidentiality agreement. It's a standard agreement but I suggest you take it home and read through it carefully. If there's anything you don't understand, just give Meagan a call and she'll explain it to you. All right?"

Julie nodded as Vanessa handed her a pen. "Why don't you get started on filling out the information for the background check while I explain a little about the company?"

Julie nodded again as she took the pen. She filled out the paper in front of her as Vanessa leaned back in her chair. "I started this company eight years ago. We employ a small group of men who are dedicated to ensuring that a woman not only enjoys their date but is treated with the utmost respect and courtesy that she deserves. If, after your date, you are unhappy in anyway, we will refund your money no questions asked. That's a guarantee."

She crossed her legs and brushed away a piece of lint from her skirt. "Unlike other escort agencies, we also provide a free-of-charge 'getting to know you' appointment. You'll meet your escort at a location of your choosing for a half hour meeting. It gives you a chance to get to know them a little better and decide if he's the appropriate one for your event. If it doesn't work out, we'll set you up with another escort of your choosing."

She paused. "Of course, as you're not looking for an escort for a particular event, I'm sure Cal will be more than appropriate for you. However, we still believe the introductory meeting is a good idea."

"Do uh, do many women use an escort for just a regular date?" Julie asked.

"Of course." Vanessa smiled at her and Julie wondered if the woman was lying. "Our clients utilize our services for many different reasons, Julie."

"Right." Julie bent her head and finished filling out the background check before handing the papers to Vanessa.

"So um, how much does this cost?" She asked awkwardly.

Vanessa gave her a thoughtful look. "We have a flat rate fee of five hundred dollars for the first four hours. Anything over four hours is charged on an hourly basis of two hundred per hour."

"Al; right." Julie, mentally calculating the cost of losing her virginity, didn't respond when Vanessa spoke to her.

"Julie?"

"I'm sorry. I was woolgathering," Julie said.

"That's fine. I was saying that payment is made directly to the company. You are not, under any circumstance, to give your escort money. All expenses will be paid by your escort and if the event lasts longer than four hours, your escort will notify us how long the event lasted, your credit card will be billed the following business day and a new invoice will be given to you. The charge on your statement will show as a numbered company, not Vanessa's Escort Agency. Clear?"

"Yes," Julie replied.

"Excellent. Take home the confidentiality agreement, read it carefully and if you agree to the terms and conditions, sign it and email it back to us. Once your background and criminal check have been cleared, we'll contact you to arrange your first meeting with Cal. All right?"

"A-all right." Julie gave her a weak smile and Vanessa patted her hand lightly.

"It's okay to be nervous, Julie. It's natural. If at any time, you change your mind just let us know."

She stood and Julie stumbled to her feet and gathered the papers and her purse. Vanessa shook her hand and walked her to the elevator. Julie let out her breath in a trembling sigh and stared at the papers in her hand.

Chapter 3

"I need your help, Court."

Court sighed and switched his cell phone to his other ear before dropping to the sofa. "Hello to you too, Cal."

"I'm serious, Court. This is an honest to God emergency." His twin brother's voice was filled with urgency.

"What is it this time?" Court asked.

"I need you to meet with one of my clients."

Court sat up. "What? No. Not a chance, Cal."

"Court please," Cal begged. "I'm on thin ice with the agency as it is and if I miss this meeting, I'll be fired for sure."

"Just reschedule the client meeting, for God's sake," Court said harshly.

"I can't. The meeting is in an hour and if I try and reschedule or cancel, Vanessa will straight out fire me."

"Jesus Christ, Cal!" Court ran his hand through his dark hair. "What is wrong with you? First you even take a job at an escort agency and now you can't even keep it? If Mom knew about this..."

"She's not going to find out," Cal interrupted impatiently. "Please, Court."

"What's so important that you can't make your — what the hell do I even call it — fuck session?"

"It's not like that, Court! I have the chance to meet with a guy, someone who can change my life, man. If this goes well, I won't even have to work at that stupid escort agency."

"What guy?" Court asked suspiciously.

"Just - don't worry about it, okay? Please, can you take my place?"

"She'll know it isn't you, Cal. There's no way I can – "

"She won't!" Cal assured him. "We're identical twins. Our own sister can't tell us apart half the time."

"I'm not having sex with some pathetic, desperate woman, Cal. I'm tired and hungry and it's been a bitch of a day. Our shipment of lumber didn't come in and we're way behind on the construction of the Stanton building. I've got two guys out with injuries and I have four meetings tomorrow."

Cal sighed heavily. "You don't have to have sex with anyone. It's an initial meeting. It'll be half an hour tops. You just have to meet her, be your usual charming self, and then go home. That's it, Court."

"Cal…"

"I am begging you. If this thing doesn't work out tonight, then I need that job at the escort agency more than ever. You know I'm drowning in debt."

"And whose fault is that? If you hadn't – "

"I know, I know. Give it a rest, would you?" Cal said wearily. "Please, Court. Half an hour, that's it. All you have to do is talk with her. She won't be expecting anything else."

Court hesitated. He suddenly wished bitterly that he hadn't answered Cal's phone call. "Cal – "

Sensing weakness, Cal forged ahead. "The woman is super cute, Court. I'll text you her picture. Who knows, you might even enjoy yourself. It's been months since you and Janine broke up. All you've done is work the last six months. C'mon, I need your help."

"Goddammit!" Court said. "You owe me, Cal. Do you hear me?"

"I know," Cal said eagerly. "I'll text you her picture and the address of the coffee shop. I'm supposed to be there in just under an hour so get your ass in the shower. And wear something nice – not your usual jeans and a t-shirt."

Before Court could reply, his twin had hung up, and he tossed his phone on to the couch beside him and groaned loudly. What the hell was he getting himself into?

* * *

"How are you feeling?"

"Nervous as hell," Julie replied. She studied herself in the mirror as she held her phone to her ear.

"Don't be nervous. What are you wearing?" Mary asked.

"Just jeans and a t-shirt. The guy already knows I'm desperate. I didn't want to look even more pathetic by dressing up for just coffee."

"What t-shirt?"

"What?" Julie frowned.

"What t-shirt are you wearing?"

"I don't know. Just a t-shirt. It's blue."

"Change into that pink shirt. The one that I bought you a couple of years ago."

"It's too small," Julie replied.

"It isn't. It makes your tits look awesome and with your dark hair and pale skin, pink is your best colour."

"Mary – "

"Change, Julie! I mean it, or I'll come to the coffee shop with the damn shirt and wrestle you into it in front of him."

"Fine!" Julie dug through her closet until she found the shirt. She dropped the phone on the bed, yanked off her shirt and struggled into the pink one. She picked up the phone as she frowned at her reflection.

"It's too small. It makes my gut look huge," she grumbled.

"No, it doesn't. Besides, he'll be too busy staring at your breasts to even notice your stomach. Now, don't overthink this all right? Just go, meet the dreamboat that is Cal, and have a good time. Think of it like your interviewing him for a job. If you don't like him, there's plenty more fish in the escort agency sea. Make sure he's the right one for you, okay?"

"Oh my God," Julie groaned. "What does it matter? I just need him to be good in bed and show me what the hell I'm supposed to do, remember? Who cares if I don't like him? Besides, he'll probably take one look at me and run screaming."

"He's already seen you," Mary said patiently. "You sent that picture to Vanessa, didn't you? That means he's seen it and obviously he likes what he sees because he's meeting with you."

"Or, he just really needs the money," Julie muttered.

"Stop it, Jules. Go and have fun. Don't think about losing your virginity to him, at least not at this meeting. Just enjoy having coffee with a good looking guy, okay?"

"Yeah, yeah. Listen, I have to go. I'm supposed to be there in half an hour and if I don't leave now, I'll be late."

"All right. Have fun, Jules." Mary made a kissing noise into the phone and hung up.

She stared at her reflection again and started to reach for the blue shirt before stopping herself. So what if this one showed off her belly? The guy would possibly be having sex with her – he'd be seeing a hell of a lot more than her stomach.

* * *

Court, slightly out of breath from his dash across the parking lot, rushed into the coffee house. He was nearly ten minutes late and he scanned the room anxiously, looking for a woman who even remotely resembled the picture Cal had sent him. Knowing his luck, the picture was ten years old and she wouldn't look anything like –

"Excuse me, Cal?" A low voice to his right had him swinging around. He stared down at the woman standing beside him. She was wearing jeans and a pink shirt and he thanked God that he hadn't listened to his brother and dressed up. He had worn his customary jeans but had swapped his t-shirt out for one of his few dress shirts.

He let his gaze travel over the woman. She was short, although at 6'4" just about everyone was short to him, and curvy in all the right places. Her shirt hugged her breasts and he had to force his gaze not to linger on them. She was wearing open-toed sandals and he could see her toes, their nails painted a soft pink, peeking out from them.

He checked out her breasts for a second time. He was a boob man, always had been and always would be, and the woman standing in front of him had an impressive rack. He could almost picture how they would look as he cupped and kneaded them.

The woman cleared her throat nervously and he tore his gaze away from her chest and to her face. To his horror she was bright red with embarrassment and looked like she was about to cry.

"I'm sorry," she whispered. "I think I should leave."

"What? No, wait." He held up his hands. "I'm Cal. You're Julie, right? I'm sorry that I'm late. Traffic was terrible and I didn't realize how long it would take me to get here. Please, forgive me."

"I – that's fine," she whispered again. She still looked like she was going to cry and he groaned inwardly. If he blew this, Cal would lose his job.

Get your shit together, Court! He berated himself fiercely.

He took a deep breath and smiled at the woman. "Let's get a coffee and talk." He put his hand in the small of her back, frowning slightly at the way she was trembling, and led her to the counter.

"What would you like?" He asked.

"Oh, um, just a latte would be fine."

Her voice was amazing. Low and husky with a warm richness to it that made his groin stir. It was a voice that practically forced a man to think about sex. To imagine hot nights and the naked flesh of a warm and willing woman underneath him and moaning her need.

He cleared his throat roughly. Jesus, he had to get control of himself.

"Great." He gave her another confident smile and ordered her latte and a black coffee for himself. They waited patiently for the coffee, neither of them speaking, before he led her to a small table near the back of the shop. It wasn't overly crowded in the shop but he had a feeling the woman wanted privacy.

Julie, her hands shaking so badly she could barely hold on to her cup, sat down with a thump. She stared down at her coffee and willed herself to calm down. Cal was even better looking in person and she felt even fatter and frumpier than usual next to him. He was like some sort of ancient God, all tanned skin and hard muscles, and she was acutely conscious of her pale skin and the way she jiggled. She took a quick peek at him.

Surprisingly, he looked as nervous as she did, and a thread of despair went through her. He obviously didn't like what he saw and was trying to figure out a way to get out of the meeting. He had been ten minutes late, she had actually been about to leave when he came rushing in the door, and he could barely look her in the eye when she had approached him.

She blinked back the tears that were threatening. So what if Cal didn't like her? She would simply find another escort who did. Although, perhaps she wouldn't aim quite so high this time. She'd find someone else who didn't look like a model with his perfect teeth and cheekbones and clear green eyes that –

His hand touched hers and she jerked and hissed with pain when coffee sloshed out on to her hand.

"Oh my God. I'm sorry." He mopped the coffee off her hand with a napkin and gave her a sheepish look. "I didn't mean to scare you. Are you okay?"

She nodded and inhaled sharply when he took her hand in his. Her hand was swallowed by his large one and as he stroked the spot where the coffee had burned her, she shivered at the feel of his rough calluses. He didn't have the hands of an escort, she thought vaguely. He had the hands of a man who worked outdoors for a living, of a man who made his money through hard labour and sweat and –

"I'm sorry, Julie. Let's start again, okay? My name is Cal. It's really nice to meet you."

"It's nice to meet you as well." She forced herself to look at him. He was giving her an easy, confident grin and she tried to return it. It came out more as a grimace than a smile and she flushed again.

"You're a little nervous, huh?" He said gently.

"Yes. I've um, I've never done this before."

"That's all right. I haven't either," he replied.

She stared at him in confusion and he grinned and winked at her. "Sorry, I was going for funny."

"Oh, of course." She gave him a more natural smile and he squeezed her hand before releasing it.

"So, what do you do for work, Julie?" He asked.

"I – I don't work," she replied softly. She could feel the blush rising over her pale skin again and she cursed inwardly.

"Are you from around here?" If he found it odd that she didn't work, it didn't show on his face.

She nodded. "Yes, I was born and raised here, actually."

"Me too," he replied. "Do you have any siblings?"

She shook her head. "No, I'm an only child. How about you?"

"A brother and sister." He took a sip of his coffee. "Being an only child, you must be close to your parents."

"My mother died when I was a baby and my father died six months ago."

"I'm so sorry. Jesus, that's rough." He gave her a look of sympathy. "Do you have any other family in the city?"

"No. My mother was an only child and my father has a sister but they weren't close. I've never even met her."

He was still giving her that look of sympathy and she forced herself to smile at him. She didn't want his pity, especially not over a dead man that she had both feared and loathed. "Are you close to your parents?"

"Yes. Actually, our entire family is close. My mom and dad both come from big families and most of them live here in the city. We have family get togethers at least once a month. It's hectic and chaotic and there's about fifty kids running amok, but it's fun."

She smiled wistfully at him. "It sounds like fun."

He took another drink of his coffee before setting it on the table. "So, what do you like to do for fun, Julie?"

"Well, I um, I like to read and I – *don't say knitting, don't say knitting* – and I like to knit."

Goddammit!

"What do you knit?" He asked politely.

"Oh, mostly scarves and hats. Sometimes I get real crazy and knit a blanket."

He laughed and she blushed again. "It's kind of an old lady hobby."

"Not at all. My mom knits." He hesitated. "Wait, that didn't come out right."

She laughed, she couldn't help it, and he grinned boyishly at her. "My mom's not that old, I swear."

"Right." She was starting to relax a little and she took another drink of coffee, happy when her hand didn't noticeably tremble.

"Who's your favourite author?" He asked.

"Stephen King."

"Me too!" He gave her a look of delight. "I used to save up my allowance to buy his books when I was a kid. I'd have to sneak them past my mom, she didn't think they were appropriate, and I'd stay up all night reading them. Scared the hell out of myself more than a few times."

She smiled as he continued. "I'm not as fond of some of his newer works. His classics though, I can't get enough of them. I've read them numerous times. Which book is your favourite?"

"The Stand."

"That's in my top five. I really loved the gunslinger series, but I hated how it ended. Did you hear they're thinking of turning it into a television mini-series? I can't see how they would manage that without destroying it. I mean, it's difficult at the best of times to turn King's work into - "

He paused and gave her a sheepish look. "Sorry, I'm running off at the mouth. Let's talk about you."

"There isn't much to say," she replied.

"I don't believe that. A pretty girl like you must have lots of great stories." He winked at her and she blushed so hard she could feel sweat breaking out on her forehead.

This wasn't working. She had no idea what to say to the incredibly gorgeous man sitting across from her and she felt like a complete and utter fraud. He was doing the best he could to make it feel like a coffee date when it really was nothing more than a work meeting for him.

She took a deep breath. She didn't want to pretend this was a date, it would only make her feel more pathetic. It was better to lay out the cards exactly as they were and let him decide if he wanted to continue or not. She didn't know if they were given a choice or not by Vanessa, but she wanted to make damn sure that the man in front of her knew exactly what she was looking for. If he wasn't interested he could simply tell her, and she would find someone else at the agency.

"Julie?" Cal gave her a look of concern. "Are you okay?"

She nodded and gathered her courage. "I am. It's just – well, I appreciate that you're trying to make me feel like this is an actual date but I'd feel better if I just told you exactly what I'm looking for."

He nodded. "All right."

"I don't know if you're allowed to say no to a client's request so I wanted to give you a heads up. If you're not interested, you can tell me right now, and I won't say a word to Vanessa. I'll just tell her that I'm not interested in you and would like to meet another escort. Okay?"

"Okay," he replied simply.

"I hired an escort because I'm a virgin and I'm looking for someone to, you know, deflower me," she blurted out and then stared anxiously at Cal.

Court stared in shock at the woman sitting across from him. He wondered for a moment if he had heard her wrong. She seemed a little shy and introverted, but there was no way a woman who looked like her could be a virgin. She had to be in her late twenties at least, and with that voice and body, how could anyone resist her?

He realized that Julie was standing and gathering her purse. He blinked in surprise and stood up, grasping her arm gently. "Julie? Where are you going?"

"It's obvious what your answer is from the look on your face." She looked close to tears yet again and he cursed himself once more.

"Julie, wait, I – "

"It's fine." She tugged timidly at his hand. "I get it and I'm not insulted, really I'm not. I'll just find someone else at the agency to uh, help me with my, um, problem. It was very nice to meet you, Cal."

He refused to let her go. "Just sit down for a minute, okay? Please, Julie."

She bit at her bottom lip and then nodded and returned to her seat. He sat down and eyed her carefully, not entirely sure she wouldn't make a break for the door.

"I'm just, well I'm a little surprised. That's all," he said softly.

She laughed bitterly. "Really? Why? Because I'm thirty? I – I've led a bit of a sheltered life. My father was very domineering and controlling and I had a hard time making friends, let alone go on a date with a man. Now that he's dead, I want to live my life."

He shook his head. "It's not because of your age. I have a hard time believing that a woman as beautiful as you has never been with a man."

She finally met his gaze, her mouth dropping open, and she stared wide-eyed at him. "I – I'm not beautiful."

"Yes, you are," he replied immediately. "I can't believe you don't see it." He let his gaze wander over her thick dark hair that fell nearly to her waist before staring at her eyes.

"You're gorgeous, Julie. Honestly. You've got amazing hair and eyes the colour of the ocean and your body is..."

He trailed off, his eyes dropping to that magnificent rack, and she crossed her arms nervously over her chest. "I know what my body is."

He frowned but let it drop as he leaned forward and captured her hand. "Julie, can I ask you a question?"

"Yes," she whispered.

"Are you sure this is what you want? What you're offering to me is a gift. Do you really want to give it to someone you barely know?"

"It's not a gift. It's a burden," she replied quickly. "You're being nice to me because you're paid to but you know as well as I do that as soon as a man finds out I'm thirty and still a virgin, he'll run screaming. I want to get rid of it and maybe learn some tips on how to," she paused and blushing, looked away from him, "please a man in bed. I – I have enough self-confidence issues as it is with being heavy, I don't want to have to worry about how I am in bed too."

She suddenly gave him a pleading look. "I'm not asking for romance or flowers or anything like that. I don't want to go on a date. I just – I just want to rid myself of the hassle of being a virgin so I can find Mr. Right."

When he didn't reply, she sighed and picked up her purse again. "I'm sorry. I don't blame you for not wanting to do this and it really is fine. I'm sure there will be someone at the agency who can help me with my problem."

He felt an odd twinge in his stomach at the thought of one of the men at the escort agency taking this beautiful, fragile woman's innocence.

"It was nice to meet you, Cal."

She was walking by him now and, without stopping to think about the consequences of his actions, he caught her by the arm and tugged her to a stop. "Stop, Julie. I'll do it."

She gave him a look of surprise. "I – you will?"

He nodded. "Yes. But on one condition."

"What do you mean?" She returned to her chair and stared tentatively at him.

"I'll do what you ask, I'll take your virginity and teach you how to please a man in bed, but only if you let me take you on a date."

"Are you serious?"

He nodded. "Yes. Let me take you on a date, Julie."

She hesitated and he could have smacked himself. "If it's about the money, I can – "

"The money isn't an issue," she interrupted. "Will we, um, have sex after the date?"

He watched the blush creep up her throat and stain her cheeks a bright red.

"If money isn't an issue, then give me two dates. The first date we'll get to know each other, and on the second date we'll sleep together. Okay?"

"Okay." She glanced at her watch. "It's been over half an hour. I'd better let you get back to work."

He stood as she did and she held out her hand. He shook it and she gave him a faint smile. "Thank you. I, uh, I'll give Vanessa a call and set something up."

"Sounds good, Julie. I'll see you soon." He shook her hand and held it a moment longer than necessary.

She took a shaky breath and gently tugged her hand free. "Bye, Cal."

She left the coffee shop and Court sat down. His heart was thudding in his chest and he rubbed at his forehead. Cal was going to kill him.

Chapter 4

"Why are you not angry with me?" Court took a large swallow of beer and stared at his brother across the table.

Cal shrugged. "Why would I be? I know you don't like to hear about my work life, but this is what I do, Court. I have sex with women for money. I would have done exactly what you did. Of course, I wouldn't have thought to sucker her into an extra 'get to know you' date, so thanks for that."

He winked at Court and took his own swallow of beer.

Court frowned at his brother. "Cal, this woman is sweet and a little fragile. Do you get that?"

"Yeah, yeah. I'll admit though — I'm not thrilled that she's never been banged before. I've done a few virgins in my time and half the time they just lie there." Cal was checking his text messages and Court gritted his teeth.

"Cal!"

"What?" Cal gave him a look of frustration.

"This is important. You need to be gentle with Julie. She's not like the usual — "

Cal laughed. "Jesus, Court. Now you're trying to give me sex tips? I hate to tell you this brother but I've got skills in the bedroom and I don't need your advice. The woman will be completely satisfied, trust me."

"That isn't what I meant," Court said through gritted teeth.

Cal was busy checking his phone again and Court raked his hand through his hair. Maybe Julie would chicken out and not even make the appointment. He kicked Cal under the table and Cal gave him an irritated look.

"What, *Courtney*?" His twin only called him by his given name when he was angry with him and Court glared at him.

"Kiss my ass, *Calvin*. Julie probably won't even set up another appointment but if she does – "

"You don't give yourself enough credit. She called Vanessa this morning and set up the appointment. I'm taking her out tomorrow night."

"What? That soon?" Court stood and paced restlessly back and forth.

"Yes." Cal gave him a curious look. "What the hell is up with you, Court?"

Court, his stomach churning, made a sudden decision. "Cal, I want you to let me take your place."

"What? Why?"

"What does it matter? I want to take your place."

"No, man. I need the money. I won't hear back from that investor guy for a couple of weeks."

Court rolled his eyes. "You can keep the goddamn money, Cal. I'm going on the dates with Julie."

"Why?" Cal asked again. "What is up with you and this chick? I've never seen you this worked up over a woman before. Is this girl like incredibly hot or something? I mean, she was cute in her picture but something's got you all hot and bothered."

"It's not like that," Court said. "In fact, I'm going to do my best to convince her not to go through with this deflowering thing."

Cal looked up from his phone. "Whoa! No you are not! I told you that I'm already on thin ice with Vanessa. If this woman calls and complains about me, Vanessa will fire my ass."

"She won't put in a complaint. Julie is very sweet and innocent, and I just want the chance to convince her that she should wait for the right man. Someone who won't think of her virginity as a burden."

"Someone like you?" Cal raised his eyebrow at him.

Court flushed. "What do you care? You'll be getting paid to sit at home and drink beer."

"Good point." Cal tipped his beer to him. "Fine. You can go on the date with Julie the Virgin but you have to promise me that you don't fuck this up. If Vanessa finds out what we're doing she won't just have me fired, she'll have my balls on a platter."

"I won't fuck it up. Give me Julie's number."

Cal shook his head. "That's not how it works. You can't call her or text her unless she gives you permission. And even if she does – trust me, it's not a good idea to contact her outside of your scheduled appointments. Very few escorts contact their clients outside of working hours. It's frowned on by the agency because it usually means you're making some extra money self-contracting, if you get what I mean."

He drained his beer and set the bottle on the table with a loud thump. "I'll text you her address. You're picking her up tomorrow at four for your 'date'. I had Meagan at the agency tell her it was casual dress. Got it?"

"I've got it," Court replied.

"One last thing - if it goes past four hours, you need to text me and let me know exactly how much longer it was. Do you understand? I'll need to send in the information to the office so they can bill her credit card the extra charge."

"Yeah, I'll let you know." Court stood and started toward the door of his brother's apartment.

"Court?"

He paused in the doorway. "Yeah?"

"Don't get me fired."

"I won't," Court said firmly. "Text me her address."

* * *

She was waiting nervously in the hallway when he rang the doorbell. She waited a beat and then opened the door. Cal smiled at her before letting his gaze drift over her body and she blushed. He was wearing jeans and a dark green t-shirt that clung to his upper body. She stared for a long moment at the bulging biceps in his arms before making herself look away.

"You look beautiful, Julie," Cal said warmly.

"Thank you. Am I – is my outfit appropriate?"

Mary had taken her shopping yesterday and helped her pick out her outfit. She was wearing a dark pink empire-style dress. It hugged her breasts and flowed loosely down her body to her knees. Mary had squealed over the way it showcased her chest but Julie had chosen it because it hid the bulge of her stomach and her thick thighs. It was autumn and a bit too cool for the sleeveless dress but she had a dark brown cardigan to wear over it. It was soft and warm and it made her more comfortable to have her arms hidden.

Mary had frowned over the cardigan, insisting that no woman wore a cardigan on a date, but Julie had refused to budge. Mary had finally allowed her to wear it when Julie promised not to button it up.

Now, Cal gave her another warm, appreciative look that made her entire body tingle. "Yes. You look amazing. Really."

"Thank you," she replied softly.

Court tried not to stare at Julie. It was obvious she was feeling self-conscious and he still couldn't believe that she didn't have at least some idea of how gorgeous she was. The dark pink of her dress highlighted the paleness of her skin, rather than washing her out, and he could hardly stop himself from touching her dark hair to see if it was as soft as it looked. She wasn't wearing makeup, just a touch of something glossy on her lips and he studied the curve of her bottom lip. He had the ridiculous urge to suck on it and he cleared his throat loudly.

"You have a lovely home," he said politely. He had been a little shocked when he'd pulled up to the address that Cal had texted him and seen the size of the house. It was a literal mansion and he peered interestedly over her shoulder at the paintings that adorned the walls of the wide hallway.

"Thanks," she said briefly. "So should we get going or..."

"Yes, absolutely. Wait – are you wearing comfortable shoes?" He glanced down at her feet. She was wearing flat sandals and he nodded his approval.

"Yup, those'll do." He held out his hand and after a brief hesitation she took it. He waited while she locked the door and then took her hand again and led her to his vehicle.

She looked in surprise at his battered truck as he opened the passenger door.

"What?" He raised his eyebrows at her.

"Nothing," she said quickly. "It's just uh, I guess I thought an escort would drive like a sports car, or something."

"That's my other car." He winked at her and she smiled shyly at him before climbing into the truck.

"So, where are we going?" She asked curiously as he drove down the street. He drove with an easy confidence and she smoothed her dress down as he turned left and accelerated.

"It's a surprise." He grinned at her. "But, if you ask me nicely I'll give you a hint."

She laughed. "Please, will you give me a hint?"

"Well, since you asked so sweetly. You'll need comfortable shoes."

She laughed again. "That's not a hint."

"Sure it is."

"It is not," she argued.

"I'll give you one more hint," he said teasingly. "A sweet tooth is required."

She mulled that over as he drove through the streets until they were on the outskirts of the city. She gasped softly at the large Ferris wheel looming in the distance.

"The fair!" She grinned delightedly at him.

"That's right." He returned her smile. "The fall fair is going on and I thought it would be fun to go. What do you think? We could always do something different if you want."

She shook her head. "No. The fair is a wonderful idea."

"Great!" He turned off the highway and she leaned forward and stared at the fairgrounds as they grew closer.

"I've never been to a fair before," she confessed.

"You're kidding."

She shook her head. "No, my father didn't approve of them. He said they were full of thieves and liars."

He didn't reply as he pulled into the large parking lot and parked the truck. The lot was already close to overflowing and she felt a mild thread of anxiety. Years of being around no one but her father had made her leery of large crowds, and she took a deep breath as Cal hopped out of the truck and crossed in front of it.

He opened her door and held out his hand. "Ready?"

She gathered her courage and took his offered hand. "Yes."

* * *

Court took Julie's hand and squeezed it lightly. "Are you getting tired?"

She shook her head. "No, not at all." She clutched the small stuffed elephant that he had won her at the ring toss game, a little closer. "I'm having a wonderful time."

"Good." He held out the bag of cotton candy. "Have some cotton candy."

She started to reach for it before dropping her hand. "I'd better not."

"Why not?" He frowned at her.

She shrugged. "I've already had a hot dog and a candy apple and I'm, you know, chubby enough."

He rolled his eyes. "Your body is perfect. Have some cotton candy, Julie."

She flushed and reached into the bag, snagging a large piece of the soft pink candy and popping it into her mouth."

"Good?"

"Yes, so good." She grinned at him like a little kid and he held the bag out to her.

"Would you like some more?"

She took another large handful and he watched as she ate the sugary candy slowly. When she was done, she licked her fingers and his cock hardened against his jeans as he watched her suck at her long fingers. He caught a hint of her small pink tongue and he could barely stop from groaning out loud.

"Cal?"

He realized with a start that Julie was saying his brother's name and he tore his gaze from her mouth. She was staring at him and her pale cheeks were flushed.

"Yes?" He prayed she wouldn't look down and see the noticeable bulge in the front of his jeans.

"Are you okay? You have a weird look on your face," she said hesitantly.

He just bet he did. He made himself smile at her before reaching in and grabbing a handful of the cotton candy. "I'm great, Julie. I'm having a really nice time."

"Me too. Thank you, Cal," she said shyly.

"You're welcome. Come on, there's one last thing we need to do before the fireworks start."

"What's that?"

"Ride the Ferris wheel of course." He grinned at her and took her hand, tugging her toward the giant wheel that lit up the night sky.

"Cal, wait. I'm not really much of a ride person," she protested as he led her forward and they stood in line.

"It'll be fine. The Ferris wheel is perfectly safe. I promise."

They were at the front of the line now and he handed the ride operator their tickets and the man opened up the gate. He held her hand firmly and led her to the brightly coloured bucket. He sat down on it and patted the seat beside him.

"Just try it, Julie. I promise it'll be worth it."

Julie took a nervous look behind her. The ride operator was giving her an impatient look and she smiled weakly at him before sitting next to Cal. His wide body took up most of the seat and she blushed with embarrassment when she had to wedge her full ass into the seat beside him. Cal smiled at her and put his arm across the back of the seat as the ride operator swung the metal bar closed and locked it.

He returned to the controls and pushed a lever. Their bucket moved with a jolt and she gave a breathless gasp of surprise. Cal rubbed her arm through her cardigan as they moved backwards into the night sky.

"You okay?"

"Y-yes," she stammered.

The Ferris wheel ground to a halt as the operator loaded the next passengers in and she squeaked with fear when their bucket rocked back and forth.

"It's fine," Cal said soothingly. He tugged her toward him and she leaned into his warmth. The air was even cooler now that the sun had gone down and he rubbed her arm again.

"Are you too cold?" He wasn't wearing a jacket but his body was deliciously warm and she leaned more firmly against him.

"No. Why?" She asked.

"The tip of your nose is red and you're trembling," he replied.

"I'm not cold," she said softly.

She was too embarrassed to admit that she was trembling from the feel of his warm, hard body against hers. She had never been this close to a man before and every nerve in her body was singing. She was acutely aware of the warmth of his thigh against hers through the thin material of her dress. Of the way his hand continued to rub her arm and the way his breath stirred her hair.

"Are you sure?" He asked.

"Yes." She made herself smile at him as the Ferris wheel slowly began to turn. She held her breath as they rose to the top and let it out in a harsh rush when the midway, its lights twinkling and gleaming in the cool air, was presented to them.

"Wow," she whispered.

She reached for his hand and he held it tightly as the wheel began its descent. They sat in silence as they rode, Julie smiling with delight every time the wheel carried them to the top. On their fourth go-around, the wheel ground to a halt as they reached the very top and Julie gasped again.

She stared around eagerly, her fear forgotten, before turning and grinning at Cal. "It's so beautiful."

"You're so beautiful," he whispered.

The hand that was stroking her arm moved upward and cupped the back of her neck beneath the soft mass of her hair. Before she could react he tugged her forward and pressed his mouth against hers.

Court groaned softly. Julie's lips were incredibly soft and when she gasped against his mouth, he threw caution to the wind and slid his tongue past her parted lips. She tasted like the cotton candy she had been eating, sweet and sugary, and he brushed his tongue against hers as she made a low and husky moan.

He cupped her face, rubbing her cheek with his thumb as he deepened the kiss. He explored her mouth with slow, careful deliberateness as she pressed her lush body against his. The bucket rocked back and forth gently and he used the motion in his kiss, pressing firmly then lightly on her mouth as the bucket swayed. She moaned and pressed harder against him, and he sucked on her lower lip before pulling back and smiling at her.

Her eyes were closed and her mouth was still parted and he rubbed his thumb across her bottom lip. She made a soft little sigh and opened her eyes, blinking rapidly at him.

"Cal, please," she whispered.

"Court," he said roughly.

She gave him a confused look. "I'm sorry?"

"My name is Court." He didn't care what happened. He couldn't listen to Julie moaning his brother's name in that husky, sexy voice.

"Court?" She was starting to pull back from him and he shifted closer to her, threading his fingers into her soft hair and holding gently.

"The agency asks us not to use our real name," he lied.

"Oh." She bit at that deliciously sweet bottom lip. "Why are you telling me your real name then? Won't you get in trouble?"

He smiled at her. "Only if you tell them I told you."

"I won't," she said solemnly. "I promise."

"I know you won't." He pressed another quick kiss against her mouth as the ride began to move again.

He sat back and she curled into him like a kitten. He took her hand and gently rubbed the palm of her hand with his thumb. She shivered delicately and then smiled shyly at him.

"Court is a different name."

He grinned widely. "My parents thought I was going to be a girl so they chose Courtney. When I was born they were a little surprised."

"So they decided to keep the name Courtney anyway?"

He gave a long suffering sigh. "My father has a unique sense of humour and my mother agreed to it when he promised to call me Court."

"And does he?" She asked.

He laughed. "Most of the time."

"I like it," she announced suddenly. "It's different and besides, you're manly enough to pull off a girl's name."

"Why thank you, little lady." He made a show of flexing his biceps in front of her and she snorted and rolled her eyes as they stopped at the bottom and the ride operator unlocked the metal bar.

Holding hands, they walked down the midway. There were still crowds of people but her escort was a big man and people naturally moved out of his way as they walked. It had been like that all afternoon and she breathed another silent prayer of thanks. The thought of being around so many strange people, the possibility of them touching her or bumping into her, had made her more anxious than she realized and it had been a relief when no one but Cal touched her.

Court, she reminded herself. *His name is Court.*

"Have you told other, um, dates what your real name is?" She asked suddenly.

He shook his head. "No."

A little thrill went through her and she made herself tamp it down. It didn't matter that he hadn't told other women his real name. She needed to remember that this was his job and sharing his real name with her didn't mean anything.

They were almost to the parking lot and she gave him a timid look. "Are you – is the date over? I thought we were going to watch the fireworks."

"We are, but I have the perfect spot to watch the fireworks. Trust me." he replied.

Smiling happily to herself, Julie followed him toward the truck.

Chapter 5

Julie climbed steadily up the hill. She knew her face was red and she tried not to pant too loudly as Court gave her an encouraging look.

"Not too much further."

She nodded, not trusting herself to speak without gasping, and continued on. Court had taken her to the truck and grabbed a blanket from the back seat before leading her across the parking lot. There was a short but steep hill looming out of the darkness in front of them, and they had climbed up through the sparse trees.

"Here we are."

They had crested the hill. Julie gave a soft gasp of surprise. Below them, the fair was spread out in a gorgeous display of shimmering lights and she collapsed with a sigh of relief on the blanket that Court laid on the soft grass.

"It's so pretty," she murmured.

Court dropped down beside her and leaned back on his elbows. "Told you it was worth it. Just wait until the fireworks start."

She could see crowds of people starting to gather at the far end of the fairground and she gave him a curious look. "How do you know about this place?"

He shrugged. "When I was a kid, my parents took us to the fair every year. My dad knew about this spot. We would sit up here and watch the fireworks without being stuck in a big crowd of people."

"I'm surprised no one else knows about it."

"Some years there are other people around so it's not a complete secret. But it's never as crowded or loud as it is down there."

He glanced around. "We got lucky tonight – it's just you and me."

"I'm glad." She blushed and thanked God he couldn't read her thoughts. She couldn't stop thinking about that kiss on the Ferris wheel. His lips had been warm and firm and he'd tasted so sweet. Just the touch of his hand against her neck had been enough to bring a strange but not entirely unwelcome warmth to her belly.

She blushed again and stared at her lap. Her nipples were hardening against her bra and the center of her was throbbing in a way she'd never felt before. She took a deep breath and closed her eyes.

"Are you okay, Julie?" Court asked.

"Yes, why?" She kept her eyes closed as he shifted closer.

"You're blushing."

"No, I'm not."

"Yes, you are." He laughed and leaned against her lightly before tracing the apple of her cheek with one rough finger. "You're practically glowing."

She sighed. "I hate how pale I am. It's awful."

He shook his head immediately. "I like your pale skin. It turns the most beautiful shade of pink whenever I touch you."

She swallowed thickly as he traced his finger down her throat and across the soft skin of her upper chest. "I wonder just how far down your blush goes."

He traced the top edge of her dress and she moaned softly in response. He eased her sweater off of her shoulders and tugged the strap of her dress and her bra down her arm before leaning forward and placing a warm, wet kiss on her shoulder. She gasped and clutched at his arms as he trailed a path of kisses across her shoulder and up her neck.

Every spot his mouth touched was lit up by a deep, smoldering fire and she twitched against him as his mouth reached her ear. He sucked lightly on the lobe and she moaned again as he whispered, "Your skin is so soft, Julie. I can't resist touching you."

His voice had deepened with something her mind didn't understand but her body reacted instantly to it. She could feel moisture gathering between her legs and her nipples were hard buttons against her bra. She squeezed her thighs together and whimpered softly when he stroked her collarbone with the tips of his fingers.

She didn't object when he pulled her sweater off completely and pushed her gently on to her back. He leaned over her and kissed her again, stroking her lips with his tongue. She opened them and he pushed his tongue into her mouth. She wrapped her arms around his broad shoulders and kissed him back.

She had kissed boys before, a few stolen kisses as a teenager here and there, but she had never been kissed like this. He took control, coaxing and teasing her mouth with his lips and tongue until she was thrusting her hips against him mindlessly.

A loud boom shook the ground as he dipped his head and kissed her neck, and the sky lit up in an explosion of blue light.

"Court," she moaned, "the fireworks have started."

"Right," he whispered. He didn't lift his head, and she stared sightlessly at the lights exploding across the sky as he licked and sucked her soft skin.

When his warm hand cupped her breast she cried out and arched her back. His thumb searched for her nipple, finding the hard pebble easily against the fabric of her dress, and he rubbed it firmly.

"Ohhhh…" she sighed as he kneaded and rubbed first one breast and then the other.

He kissed her again, his tongue thrusting into her mouth as he pushed his thigh between hers. She spread her legs willingly, squeezing them around his hard leg. When he rubbed his thigh against her hot core, she moaned and thrust her pelvis at him.

He groaned against her mouth and his hand tightened around her breast. Hesitantly she reached down and slid her hands under his t-shirt. His skin was hot and he made another loud groan when she traced her fingers across his rock-hard abs.

She wanted to see his chest, wanted to see the warm flesh she was tracing, and she pulled timidly at the hem of his shirt. Despite the cool air, he immediately pulled off his shirt and tossed it to the side. She stared at his chest and slowly traced her fingers through the dark hair.

He inhaled sharply and she squeaked in surprise when he pulled her into a sitting position. He pulled down the zipper on her dress and reached for the clasp of her bra as her fingers pressed tightly into his chest.

"Court, I – "

"I need to see them, Julie," he murmured. "I need to see your breasts. Please, darlin'."

She bit at her lip and then gave a quick, short nod. She was feeling shy and uncertain but this was what she had hired Court for. He undid the clasp with a practiced flick and pulled her bra straps and dress straps down off of her arms. She reached to clutch the bodice of her dress to her chest but his hands beat her to it and with a quick tug he pulled the material to her waist. She automatically crossed her arms over her naked breasts, embarrassment flooding through her, and he took her arms and tugged them down.

"No, darlin'. I want to see you."

She closed her eyes, afraid to see the look on his face, and after a moment he touched her face. "Open your eyes, Julie."

Her eyelids fluttered open and she stared mutely at him.

"You're so beautiful. Do you hear me?" He caressed her cheek with his fingers.

"I'm not," she whispered.

"You are," he insisted. His gaze dropped to her naked breasts. They were ripe and full with pale pink nipples that were hard and begging for his mouth. He groaned and abruptly pushed her on to her back.

"Court, what – oh my God!" She cried out with pleasure when his hot, wet mouth closed around her nipple.

"Oh!" She cried again as he sucked firmly on her nipple before tracing the tip with his tongue. Her hands clung to the blanket beneath her for a moment before she reached up and threaded her fingers into his thick hair. She clutched at his head as he laved at her nipple. Small breathless cries escaped from her mouth as she twisted beneath him.

He slid his hand up under her dress and trailed his fingers along her thigh. His fingers touched the waistband of her panties and then his hand was slipping under them and cupping her warm pussy.

She gave him a wide-eyed look of desire mixed with uncertainty, and he stroked the soft hair at the apex of her thighs before sliding his finger between the lips of her pussy. Her clit was swollen and hard and he rubbed it gently, watching her face.

"Such a wet little pussy," he whispered. "I love how wet you are, Julie."

"Oh my God," she moaned and arched her hips against Court's hand. He dropped his mouth to hers and she kissed him frantically as his fingers stroked and caressed her throbbing clit.

She panted and moaned, her hips rising and falling with the touch of his fingers. The muscles in her pelvis were tightening to a fevered pitch, and she gave him another of those wide-eyed looks as he smiled down at her.

"Court, it feels — I mean, I don't know what's happening. Please!" She suddenly cried.

He rubbed harder, his fingers dancing over her clit until she thought she would go mad. Sparks of pure pleasure were running up and down her legs, and she moved them restlessly as her hands clutched at his hard biceps.

"Relax and let it happen, darlin'," he murmured into her ear.

She didn't reply. She was beyond speech, beyond the ability to even think clearly, and she moaned and writhed and bucked beneath him as he dipped his head and sucked on one tight nipple. She stiffened beneath him, her pelvis lifting off the blanket as she gave a loud cry of pleasure and came all over his hand.

She collapsed against the blanket, panting loudly and staring at the fireworks flashing across the sky as Court kissed her lightly on the mouth.

"You okay, darlin'?" He asked.

She nodded, still panting loudly, and gave him an odd look of embarrassment.

"I'm sorry," she whispered.

"Sorry?" He frowned at her. "For what?"

"I — I don't know," she murmured. "For being so um -
"

She didn't know what to say, she was already feeling embarrassed about her lack of control, of her absolutely wanton behaviour with him, but she didn't know how to express it.

"For being so loud," she finished lamely.

He grinned and kissed the tip of her nose. "I like loud. It lets me know I'm doing something right."

She blushed and watched as he grimaced and tugged at the front of his jeans. Another wave of embarrassment went through her. She had been so focused on what he was doing to her that she hadn't even thought of his need.

Feeling unsure about what she was supposed to do, she reached down and placed her hand on the bulge she could see at the front of his jeans. His breath hissed out between his teeth and giving him a nervous smile, she rubbed it firmly.

He groaned and arched his body into her hand as his eyes closed and his hand came up to cup her breast. She was surprised to feel a new pulse of pleasure grow in her belly at the feel of his erection and the obvious need on his face.

She continued to rub, feeling nervous but determined to make him feel as good as he had made her. He groaned, louder this time, and pinched her swollen nipple. She gasped and reached for his belt.

"Jesus, Julie," he muttered and jerked against her. "You have no idea what you do to me."

"I'm sorry," she whispered, her hand stilling on his belt buckle.

He shook his head. "You have nothing to be sorry about but we should probably get going."

He sat up and pulled on his t-shirt before helping her into her bra and dress. Her face bright red, she stared at the ground as he tugged her to her feet and neatly folded the blankets. The air was cold and away from his warm body, she was beginning to shake.

Court tucked the blanket under his arm and held out his hand to Julie. "Ready?"

She nodded and he frowned at the look on her face. "Julie? What's wrong?"

"Nothing's wrong," she said quickly.

He pulled her into his embrace and stroked her hair. "Yes, there is. Tell me."

She stared at his chest. "I thought we were going to – I mean, you didn't even…"

She trailed off and stared miserably up at him. "Did I do something wrong when I was – was touching you?"

He shook his head and kissed her lightly on the mouth. "No, not at all. It's just that it's getting colder and we're out in the open. I don't want your first time to be outdoors on a blanket with the possibility of someone stumbling upon us."

"Are you sure it wasn't something I did?"

"Positive." He kissed her again. "I liked everything you did to me, Julie."

She smiled and he took her hand. "Come on, let's get you home before you freeze to death."

Chapter 6

Julie stared at the front of her dark house. She didn't want to go alone into that giant, empty house filled with nothing but memories of her father belittling her. What she wanted was to bring Court with her, to take him to her bed and have him touch her and bring her the same pleasure he had brought her earlier.

She was thirty years old and she'd just had her very first orgasm. She knew that other women in their teens and twenties had experimented with their bodies, using their own touch to find pleasure, but she never had. She had been too afraid her father would hear her. Afraid that he would somehow know what she was doing and ridicule her even further. That he would use it as further proof that she would be alone forever.

Now, only half an hour after her first sweet taste of pleasure, she was craving it again. Her core – *pussy*, she thought, *let's not be coy, it's your pussy* – was aching and throbbing and she was acutely aware of Court's scent, of his overwhelming, thoroughly intoxicating maleness, and she wanted him desperately.

Taking a deep breath, she turned to face him. "Would you like to come in? I could make you coffee or…something."

He glanced at his watch. "I'd better not, Julie. It's getting pretty late."

Her stomach dropped and she nodded. "Right, of course. Good night, Court. Thank you, I had a lovely time."

Her face burning, she reached for the door handle. Faintly, she could hear Court cursing and then he was sliding across the seat and pulling her into his arms. He kissed her firmly, his tongue sliding into her mouth and cutting off her protest.

After a few heady moments, he pulled back. He was panting lightly and his eyes were dark with need. "You really don't understand how much I want to come into your house with you, Julie. How badly I want to carry you to your bed, strip off your clothes and sink my cock deep into your warm, tight pussy."

Her breath rushed out of her in a trembling sigh and she stared at him. She had never been so turned on in her life, and she wondered if he would find it strange if she asked him to repeat his words.

He sighed harshly and rested his forehead on hers as she stroked his back. "I want that too, Court. So come inside with me."

"You promised me two dates, remember?" He replied. "Next time, I'll come in."

"Do you promise?" She whispered.

He nodded. "Yes. Now," he kissed her again, a sweet and gentle one that sent shivers down her spine, "you'd better go before I change my mind."

"Good night, Court."

"Good night, Julie."

* * *

"So? How did it go? Did you convince the sweet little virgin to keep her legs closed?"

Cal was sitting on his couch, drinking a beer and eating a sandwich, when Court let himself into his apartment.

"Why are you eating my food?" He dropped his keys on the side table and pulled off his boots before collapsing on the couch next to his brother.

Cal shrugged. "I was hungry and I didn't have any food at my place. So – did you convince her?"

Court flicked on the TV and stared at the screen. At the start of the date he'd had every intention of convincing Julie that she didn't want to lose her virginity to him. But that was before he had kissed her. Before he had tasted the sweetness of her lips and heard her husky moans of need. He had lost control tonight and when Julie had invited him in, he had come very close to just saying 'fuck it' and joining her in her bed.

He wanted Julie. He hardly knew her, and two days ago he'd had no desire to be in any kind of relationship – thanks to Janine – but there was something about her that called to him. He decided it was a combination of her sweetness and her fragility that appealed to him. He had never met anyone like her before, and he was a little alarmed by the feelings of protectiveness she brought out in him.

"Earth to Court? Hey? Did you convince her?" Cal nudged him with his foot and Court gave him a dirty look.

"None of your business, Cal."

Cal arched his eyebrow and took a large bite of the sandwich. "None of my business?" He mumbled around the bread. "Interesting."

"What's that supposed to mean?"

Cal shrugged. "Only that it's easy to tell when you actually like a woman because you refuse to talk about it. You've gone on one date with this chick and technically, she paid you to do it. I mean, I'm getting the money but still..."

He dropped his sandwich on the plate sitting on his lap and fished out his cell phone. "That reminds me." He checked the time and sent off a quick text.

"What are you doing?" Court asked.

"Letting Vanessa know what time the date finished. You went longer than the four hours, little brother."

Court rolled his eyes. "I was born two minutes after you, Cal. Give the little brother thing a rest, would you?"

Cal laughed and pinched his cheek. "You'll always be my baby brother."

"Knock it off!" Court punched him in the arm and Cal winced before picking up his sandwich again.

"So, you obviously like this woman. Can I assume that you took care of the poor woman's virginity problem?"

Court didn't answer and Cal sighed. "Just let me know if I should be expecting another date with her or not."

"Yes. One more," Court replied.

"Just one?"

"Yes," he said shortly.

Cal studied him for a moment. "All kidding aside, Court, I think you should take a step back. Nothing's going to happen between you and this woman, you know that right? I mean, she's paying you – me – to take her virginity. She obviously doesn't want a relationship with a man. If she did, she'd be out there hitting the bars like a normal woman."

"She's perfectly normal!" Court snapped. "She's just shy and embarrassed that she's a virgin at thirty."

"Thirty!" Cal whistled. "Jesus, she really is an old maid."

"Shut up, Cal," Court said warningly.

"Well, why the hell is she still a virgin? She's not ugly. In fact, she's pretty cute. Did you ask her why she hasn't bumped uglies with someone?"

Court sighed. "She alluded to her dad being pretty controlling and it sounds like he did a pretty good number on her self-esteem. She thinks she's ugly."

Court took another bite of his sandwich and chewed noisily before swallowing. "You do know that you can't have a relationship with her, right? Even if you convinced her to date you outside of the escort agency, she thinks you're me. What do you think she'll do when she finds out you've been lying to her?"

"I know, Cal!" Court replied grumpily. "I don't want a relationship with her. I just want to stop her from doing something she'll regret."

"Which is why you're going on a second date with her?"

"Yes."

"So you'll convince her to save herself for marriage or her one true love or whatever, and then you'll never see her again. Is that right?"

"Yes," he repeated firmly.

Cal laughed. "You let me know how that works out for you, baby brother."

* * *

"Oh, Julie," Mary breathed quietly, "you look gorgeous."

Julie gave her an earnest look. "Do you really think so?"

Mary stood up from Julie's bed and turned her around so she was facing the full length mirror.

"Are you kidding me, Jules? You're a goddamn knockout. He's not going to know what hit him."

Julie stared at herself. She was wearing a dark blue dress that hugged her full figure. The skirt was above her knees and she pulled a little self-consciously at it before studying her cleavage. The neckline was very low and, thanks to the push-up bra she was wearing, a ridiculous amount of her breasts was showing. She had never worn something so revealing before and she tried to tug the neckline of the dress up with one hand while pulling at the bottom of the dress with the other.

Mary slapped at her hands and tugged the neckline back to its proper spot. "Leave it, Jules."

"It's too low, Mare. My nipples are almost showing," she protested.

Mary laughed and slapped her lightly on the ass. "No, they're not. Now, come sit down and let me finish your make-up."

She led Julie to the attached bathroom and pulled a pack of eye shadow from the bag sitting on the counter. She closed the toilet lid and motioned for Julie to sit down. Julie perched carefully on the toilet before giving Mary a look of horror. "The dress is too short! The top of my stockings are showing."

Mary laughed. "They'll be hidden under the table. Don't worry about it. Just, for God's sake, if you drop something remember to squat not bend to pick it up."

She carefully brushed the shadow on to Julie's eyelids. "So," she said casually, "you never really gave me the details of your first date with Cal. How did it go?"

"Good. He took me to the fair and won me the cutest stuffed elephant. We walked around and he took me on the Ferris wheel. I've never been on one before."

"I know you haven't," Mary said gently. She used a larger brush to apply blush to Julie's cheeks. "What else did you do?"

"We climbed to the top of this hill – oh god, Mare, I was panting so loudly it was embarrassing – and then we talked for a bit. Court said – "

"Court?" Mary interrupted.

"Oh, uh..." Julie gave her a nervous look. "The agency asks them not use their real names but Court told me his real name."

"Did he?" Mary said in a neutral voice.

"Uh-huh. I promised I wouldn't tell anyone though so don't let it slip when he gets here tonight, okay? Anyway, we watched the fireworks from the top of the hill and then he took me home," Julie replied.

"That was it?" Mary asked.

"Yes," Julie lied.

Mary gave her a scrutinizing look. "Did you know that when you're lying, your left eye twitches?"

"It does not!" Julie protested.

"Yes, it does. It's why I can always tell when you're lying. Even when we were kids, Jules."

Julie blushed and licked her lips as Mary arched her eyebrows at her. "Did you have sex with him?"

"No," Julie replied.

"What did you do?" Mary prompted gently.

"We – we kissed and made out a little during the fireworks," Julie replied. She loved Mary but she wasn't going to give her the exact details of what had happened. She wanted to keep that memory to herself. It was too sweet and special to share."

"Did you enjoy it?"

"Yes, very much." Julie couldn't stop the grin from crossing her face.

"So why didn't you sleep with him?" Mary asked.

"Court asked me to give him two dates. He wants to make sure this is, you know, what I really want to do."

Mary frowned. "Sounds like an easy way to make some extra money. String you along by pretending he's concerned about you."

Julie shook her head. "No, it's not like that. He said he would take my virginity on the second date if that was what I wanted."

"And is it?"

"Yes. The way Court makes me feel, I've never felt anything like it before." She blushed and gave Mary a nervous look. "I want him so badly, Mare."

Mary was giving her an odd look and she set the make-up brush down before crouching and taking Julie's hands. "Jules, you're not falling for this guy, are you?"

"What?" Julie shook her head quickly. "No, of course not."

"That's good because, honey, you know he doesn't care for you, right? I mean, it doesn't sound like he's cold-hearted and he's obviously got morals, but you haven't forgotten he's being paid for this, have you?"

"No, I haven't, Mary," Julie said a bit crossly and pulled her hands free. "I might be naïve and a bit clueless but I'm not stupid. I know Court is only being nice to me because I'm paying him to."

"That isn't what I meant," Mary said soothingly. "I just meant that it's not a good idea to get too attached to this guy."

"This was your idea. Remember, Mary? Get my stupid v-card out of the way so I could find someone to have a relationship with. Are you telling me that I shouldn't go through with it now because Court is a nice guy?"

"No, not at all," Mary replied. "But," she took Julie's hands again and held them tightly, "don't get attached to him, all right? Just keep a level head and remember that you're going to sleep with this guy so that you can find someone to have a real relationship with. You don't want to go thinking that you can have a relationship with an escort. That isn't going to happen, honey."

"I know it isn't," Julie said firmly. "Now, hurry up and finish. Court will be here any minute."

* * *

Court straightened his tie before ringing the doorbell. Julie had called the day after the fair and set up an appointment for tonight. Cal had asked what he wanted to do and Court had directed him to tell Julie he would be taking her out for a formal dinner.

The door opened and he stared in surprise at the slim redhead standing in front of him. "Oh, hi. I was looking for Julie?"

"Come on in. You're Cal, right?" The woman replied.

"Yes." He stood in the hallway as the woman looked him up and down.

"My name is Mary. I'm Julie's best friend."

"It's nice to meet you." He shook her hand and she led him down the hallway and into the living room.

"It's nice to meet you too. Julie will be right down."

"Thanks."

"You bet. Can I get you a drink?" Mary asked.

He shook his head. "No, thank you. I – "

He stopped, his eyes widening as he looked behind Mary's shoulder.

Mary turned to see Julie standing in the doorway. "Hello, doll."

"Hi, Mary. Hi, Cal."

"Hello, Julie." He didn't recognize his own voice. It was hoarse with need and desire and he cleared his throat as Mary gave him a knowing grin.

Julie, dressed in a form-fitting blue dress and heels, looked like a goddess. He licked his lips and tried not to stare at the gorgeous amount of cleavage on display as Mary grinned again and picked up her purse.

"Well, I'm going to head out. Have fun, Jules." She kissed Julie on the cheek before nodding to Court and leaving. They heard the front door close and Julie gave Court a nervous smile.

"How are you?"

"Speechless."

"Is that good or bad?" She asked.

"Good. Very, very good. You look amazing, Julie." He walked toward her and had to stop himself from tracing his fingers over her exposed cleavage.

"Thank you, Court." She flushed prettily at the dark look of desire he was giving her.

He took a deep breath and looked away from her, desperate for a distraction that would stop him from pushing her to the couch and taking her right there. Her dark hair was sleek and shiny and her lips were painted a soft red, and he couldn't stop taking quick peeks at her cleavage. He took another deep breath and stuck his hands into his pockets.

"You have a really nice home."

"Thank you." She hesitated. "Would you like a tour before we leave?"

"Sure." He checked his watch. "We've got plenty of time before our reservation."

"All right. Well, this is the living room."

He took a quick look around the room before following her down the hallway to the kitchen.

"This is the kitchen – obviously." She gave a nervous laugh.

"It's very… shiny."

She laughed and inspected the gleaming white cupboards and the stainless steel appliances. "Yes, it is."

He followed her from room to room, admiring each of them, until they reached a doorway at the end of the hallway.

"This was my father's study." She opened the door but didn't go in and he stuck his head in and peered around. It was a large room, dominated by a mahogany desk in the middle of the room. He peered at the painting above the fireplace. It was of a man and a little girl and they wore identical looks of solemnity. It was easy to see that the little girl was Julie, and he studied her carefully before his gaze switched to the man.

"Holy shit," he said suddenly. "Your father is Peter Winslow?"

She nodded and he gave her a look of surprise. "Peter Winslow, the artist?"

"Yes. You know his work?"

"I do. I'm a big admirer of it, actually." As a child he had always been fascinated by art and had taken a few art classes throughout the years.

He glanced at her. "I thought I recognized the paintings in the hallway."

"They were all painted by my father."

He stared thoughtfully at her for a moment. "Your father was very well-known."

"He was," she acknowledged. "He did very well for himself."

"Very well for himself?" He grinned a little. "Your father was a goddamn millionaire."

"Yes." She hesitated. "Now you know why I don't work."

"I guess you don't need a job when you're the daughter of a millionaire."

"I didn't," she said simply. "But I wanted to work." She was suddenly afraid that he would think her lazy. "After I finished high school I wanted to become an architect."

"Why didn't you?"

"The university I wanted to attend was in another state and my father didn't want me moving so far away. He would have been, you know, lonely," she said awkwardly.

"Right." He followed her as she closed the door and started up the large staircase in front of them.

"Do you like to paint?"

She laughed a little bitterly. "No, I'm afraid I didn't get any of my father's artistic gifts. I can barely draw a stick figure. You can imagine how disappointed he was by that."

She led him through the maze of hallways, showing him room after room. Many of them were either completely empty or the furniture was covered in dust cloths.

"Christ, this house is huge," he muttered after she led him down yet another hallway.

"It is," she agreed. "Too big for one person."

"Why don't you sell it?"

She shrugged. "My father would be horrified if I sold it."

The walls were lined with more of her father's work and he studied each one carefully as they walked down the hallways. She stopped and smiled at him. "Do you like to paint, Court?"

"I do," he confessed. "I even thought about majoring in art after high school."

"Why didn't you?"

He shrugged. "I fell in with a bad crowd for a few years. Nothing too serious. I didn't go to jail or anything like that, but I smoked some weed and drank too much and generally sat around on my ass doing nothing."

"Really?"

He nodded. "Yeah. It would have gotten much worse but my dad - he's not one for just sitting by idly watching his children destroy their futures - he took me away to our cabin in the mountains for a few months. I didn't want to go. I was twenty-two and hotheaded and stupid, but he tied me up and drove me up there. Once we were there, it was either stay with dad at the cabin or die trying to get off the mountain."

"He tied you up?" She was giving him a shocked look and he grinned a little.

"Yup. Don't worry - I didn't go all mountain man crazy or anything like that. In fact, it was just what I needed to get my head straight. Anyway, after I came back I needed some money to pay off my debt so I started working construction for a few years."

He stopped as Julie looked at him expectantly. He had started his own construction company just over two years ago and although he wasn't rich, he did okay for himself. He had actually broke even this year and if he continued at his current pace he might make a profit next year. He couldn't tell any of that to Julie though so he just cleared his throat and smiled at her.

"Construction doesn't pay a whole lot so I started doing this to supplement my income."

"So you still do construction?" She asked.

He hesitated and unable to completely lie to her, nodded his head. "Yes. Not as much as I used to but, yeah."

She smiled. "I thought you worked outside."

"How did you know?"

She took his hand and stroked the calluses that were on it. "Your hands."

He laughed. "Yeah, I've got rough hands."

She blushed. "I don't mind. I think they're nice."

She gave him a look of such earnest desire that he had to take a step back before he pushed her up against the wall and kissed her. She quickly masked the look of disappointment that crossed her face and continued to the next room.

"This is my bedroom."

He stepped into the room and stared curiously around. Unlike the rest of the rooms that had a cold and almost sterile feel to them, this one was warm and inviting. It was painted a deep yellow and the walls were adorned with colourful prints. A large multi-coloured quilt hung on the wall above her bed.

"That's nice." He motioned to the quilt.

"Thank you. My mother made it while she was pregnant with me."

He didn't reply. His gaze had dropped to her bed. She hadn't made it and he stared at the rumpled sheets and the slight indent in her pillow. Her nightgown, a flimsy yellow piece of silk, was lying on the foot of her bed. His cock hardened in his pants as he imagined Julie wearing it. He could almost see her lying in her bed, dressed only in that wisp of fabric, and waiting for him. It was too easy to imagine climbing into her bed and curling up next to her warm body. Too easy to picture her arms wrapping around him while he kissed and caressed every inch of her naked skin.

"Court?" She laid a soft hand on his arm. "Are you okay?"

He nodded and made himself look at her. She inhaled sharply and his eyes dropped to her chest. She was breathing rapidly, her breasts rising and falling in that magnificent dress, and her hand tightened on his arm.

"We should go," he said thickly.

"I – I don't want to," she whispered. She stepped closer and pressed her supple body firmly against him.

"Julie," he groaned, "we should have dinner and talk first."

"Talk about what?" She bit her bottom lip and then leaned in and placed a soft, warm kiss on his throat.

His hands gripped her full hips briefly before moving to her ass and squeezing hard. She moaned and clung tightly to him before kissing his throat again.

"We need to talk about what you're asking me to do." He could barely think past the desire coursing through his veins. "Are you sure – absolutely sure – that this is what you want?"

She nodded immediately. "I'm sure. Please, Court. I want you to be my first."

He took a deep breath and she pressed a soft and trembling kiss on his mouth. "Show me how to make you feel good, Court."

He groaned and captured her mouth with his. He thrust his tongue past her lips as she pushed his suit jacket off his shoulders and yanked at his tie. He stepped back just long enough to pull his tie over his head before unbuttoning his shirt and letting it join his jacket on the floor.

She stared at his naked chest, her lips trembling, as she eyed the taut muscles of his abdomen. Her eyes drifted lower, to his erection pushing noticeably against his pants, and she swallowed.

"You want me."

"Of course I do," he whispered. "I'd have to be dead not to want you in that dress."

She smiled. "So you like it?"

"Very much so." He reached around her and stroked the zipper with his fingers. "But I think I'll like this dress better when it's on the floor."

She laughed and he grinned at her. "Was that line too cheesy?"

"Maybe a little," she said.

He pulled down the zipper and then slowly peeled down her dress. He pushed it past her hips and it fell to the floor. She stepped out of it and stared anxiously at him.

She had gone shopping earlier and Mary had helped her pick out some lingerie. Not used to a garter and stockings, she had almost balked at wearing them but Mary had convinced her to try them. Now, seeing the look on Court's face, she was very glad that she had.

"Court?" She whispered.

"Jesus Christ," he muttered. "You're killing me, darlin'."

She giggled a bit nervously as he pulled her against his body. "Are you sure, Julie?"

"Yes," she said immediately. She took his hand and led him to her bed. "Lie down with me, Court."

Before she could lie down, Court caught her by the hand. He lifted it to his mouth and kissed the palm of it lightly. A shiver started down her spine and she moaned loudly when he sucked her index finger into his mouth. He ran his tongue across her flesh and she gave him a naked look of desire.

He kissed her palm again and reached behind her to unclasp her bra. He pulled it from her body and dropped it to the floor. He bent and she arched her back, desperate for his warm mouth, but he winked again at her and dropped to his knees on the floor in front of her. He kissed her thigh, tracing the edge of her stocking with his tongue as she wound her fingers in his hair and pulled lightly.

"Court, hurry."

"We have all night, darlin'," he murmured. His hands trembling lightly, he unclipped each of her stockings and rolled them down her legs, following the downward path of the nylons with his mouth and tongue.

She stepped out of her shoes and he pulled the stockings free of her feet. He placed a light kiss on her foot and she giggled and jerked her foot away. He grinned up at her.

"Ticklish?"

"A little."

He kissed her ankle and then placed soft kisses up her left leg until his mouth was hovering over her panty-covered pussy.

"Court," she moaned as she felt his hot breath.

"Patience, darlin'." He pressed his mouth against her panties and she cried out, her entire body trembling as she pulled again on his hair.

He smiled and stood up, cupping her breast before kissing her hard on the mouth. She kissed him back, throwing her arms around him and pressing her body against his. He groaned at the feel of her hard nipples pushing into his chest and he quickly unbuckled his belt and tore at the button on his pants, raking down the zipper and pushing his pants to the floor.

"Lie on the bed, Julie," he whispered.

She lay down as he pulled off his pants and socks. She was staring at his erection and a look of anxiety crossed her face. Leaving his briefs on, he lay on his side next to her and cupped her breast gently.

"If you want to stop at any point, just tell me," he said quietly. "We can stop at any time."

She shook her head and, her face reddening, reached out and cupped his erection. "I don't want to stop, Court."

He kissed her again as he plucked gently at both of her nipples until she was moaning into his mouth and arching her back. He leaned down and licked a slow path between her breasts, tasting and teasing her soft skin as she panted heavily and moved restlessly against the sheets.

He sucked hard on one tight, pink nipple and traced the delicate skin with his tongue before sliding his hand into her panties. He rubbed at her clit and she parted her legs eagerly.

"That feels so good," she moaned.

He sucked firmly on her nipple then pinched her clit lightly. She cried out loudly, her body arching up off the bed and clutched at his arm. "Oh – oh my God!"

He licked his way to her ear and sucked on the lobe before whispering, "Do you want to come, Julie?"

"Yes! Oh yes, please!" She moaned.

"I love watching you come. Do you know that? You look so pretty with your legs spread wide and your nipples hard," he murmured.

His warm breath, naughty words, and rough fingers were driving her mad. The now-familiar pleasure was coursing through her body and with a loud cry she arched her hips as her climax burst through her.

"So very pretty," he murmured as she collapsed against the sheets. She turned to face him, kissing him hard on the mouth as she grasped his cock through his underwear. She rubbed him tentatively as she watched his face.

"I want to see you," she said softly.

He helped her yank his underwear down his hips. He pushed them off his legs as she stared at his cock. It was large and thick, and a look of anxiety crossed her face before she took a deep breath and curled her fingers around him.

He groaned and she touched him gently, her fingers tracing small circles on his throbbing shaft, before giving him a tentative look. "Does that feel good, Court?"

"Yes," he said hoarsely. "You have no idea how good."

She stroked him more firmly, his low moans making her bold, before she leaned forward and kissed his warm chest. Wondering if his nipples were as sensitive as hers, she licked the right one with the tip of her tongue and squeaked with surprise when his hips jerked against her hand and he suddenly pushed her on to her back.

"I'm sorry." She gave him another anxious look. "Did I do something wrong?"

"Christ, no," he groaned. "But I'm going to come all over your hand if you keep touching me."

He kissed her lightly. "Do you want to keep going, Julie? Tell me now if you want to stop."

"I don't want to stop," she said with a touch of impatience. "I told you that, Court."

He grinned at her tone and kissed the tip of her nose. "All right, darlin'."

He sat up and she pulled at his arm. "Where are you going?"

"I need to get a condom from my wallet."

She opened the drawer of her bedside table. "I bought some earlier today. Always be prepared, right?" She laughed nervously as she pulled out the foil wrapper and he took it from her before holding her hand.

"We can stop."

"I know." She gave him a cross look. "And I told you I didn't want to."

"Yes, you did." He pulled her back down on the bed. "I'm very happy about that, by the way."

"You are?" She asked hesitantly.

"Yes." He stroked her face lightly. "I've wanted you from the moment I saw you, Jules. It's been driving me crazy."

She shuddered with pleasure at the sound of his deep voice saying her nickname. "We only met like four days ago, Court."

"I know," he whispered. "And I've spent most of those four days trying to hide my erection from the general public."

She laughed delightedly and stroked his chest. "I want you too."

He cupped her breast and used his thumb to stroke her nipple into an unbearable hardness. The pleasure was building inside of her again and she spread her legs and pushed his hand between her thighs.

"What's this?" He whispered before pulling teasingly on her panties. "I think it's time we took these off, don't you?"

"Yes, definitely," she breathed. His mouth wrapped around her nipple and she could barely concentrate on pushing her panties down her legs. He reached down and helped untangle them from her feet before pressing his hand back between her legs.

"You're so wet, darlin'," he rasped against her breast. "I can't wait any longer."

"Me either," she moaned as his fingers danced across her throbbing, swollen clit.

She heard the rustle of the wrapper as he rolled the condom onto his cock before tugging gently on her thighs.

"Spread your legs, darlin'."

She parted her legs eagerly and he knelt between them, shifting them a little further apart before propping himself up on his arms above her.

She could feel his cock pressing against her but she felt no fear, only a demanding sense of urgency, and she thrust her hips at him. He groaned and took a deep breath before reaching before them and guiding his cock to her wet entrance.

She squeezed his arms and stared at his face as he pushed the head of his cock into her. He stopped and gave her an anxious look. "Okay?"

"Yes. Please, Court," she whispered.

He bent his head, kissing her deeply on the mouth as he entered her in one hard thrust. She winced at the sharp bite of pain and he gave her another anxious look. "I'm sorry."

"Don't be," she whispered before kissing him. "I'm fine."

"Tell me when you're ready." He stroked her hair back from her face.

"I'm ready." She shifted experimentally against him. "You don't need to wait."

Not quite believing her, he waited a few more seconds before beginning to move within her. She smiled encouragingly and gripped his waist tightly.

"Raise your knees and plant your feet on the bed, Jules," he whispered against her mouth.

She complied eagerly and he groaned as he sunk fully into her warm, wetness. He thrust back and forth, forcing himself to go slowly. It was nearly impossible. Her pussy was incredibly tight and warm and he wanted to bury himself deep within her.

"Does it – am I doing this right?" She suddenly asked.

"God, yes," he muttered. "You feel so good, Jules. You're so tight and wet."

She stroked her back with the tips of her fingers. "I want you to move faster."

He shook his head. "I don't think that's a good idea, darlin'."

"It is." She pouted at him. "Faster, Court." She bucked her hips and he thrust roughly into her in response.

She gave a soft moan of pleasure and clung tightly to him as he plunged in and out of her. He was growing close to coming already and with an almost painful groan, he reached between them and rubbed frantically at her clit.

Her reaction was strong and immediate. Her fingers dug into his ribs and she shoved her pelvis at him as he bent his head and kissed her deeply. She shuddered and moaned beneath him and he tore his mouth from hers and cried out hoarsely when she came apart around him. Her pussy tightened exquisitely around his cock, pulling his orgasm from him, and he thrust hard into her before collapsing against her soft body.

She was panting lightly and she stroked his hair as he buried his face in her damp throat. After a moment he moved reluctantly away from her, disposing of the condom before lying down next to her and covering them both with the sheet and blanket.

"Jules?" He stroked her shoulder and arm.

"Hmm?" She murmured.

"Are you okay?"

"Yes. Better than okay," she replied in a dreamy little voice. "Just sleepy."

He grinned and turned her on her side before spooning her. He cupped her breast and kissed her neck before whispering in her ear, "Thank you, darlin'."

"For what?" She asked sleepily.

"For giving me such a sweet gift," he whispered into her ear.

She murmured something unintelligible and curled deeper against his hard body. He kissed the top of her head and closed his eyes. For the first time in a long time, he was content.

Chapter 7

He sat up, scrubbing his hand across his face, before squinting blearily at her side of the bed. It was empty and he felt an odd moment of fear before he realized she was in the shower. The water turned off and he relaxed against the pillows. She crept into the bedroom, wearing a thick robe and her long dark hair piled into a messy bun on the top of her head. She moved quietly toward the door and squeaked in surprise when he cleared this throat.

"Where are you going, darlin'?"

"I – I was just thirsty."

He frowned at the anxiety in her voice and climbed naked out of the bed. She glanced at his cock, her cheeks turning pink, as he strode toward her.

"You must be hungry as well." He put his arm around her waist and nuzzled her neck.

"I'm sorry. I made us lose our dinner reservation," she said breathlessly.

He kissed her throat. "It was worth it."

"Yeah?" She gave him another anxious look and he nodded immediately.

"Yes, Jules. More than worth it."

She took a deep, trembling breath and he frowned at her. "Tell me what's wrong."

"Nothing." She smiled at him. "I guess, I just – I mean, I don't know what we do now. Do I say thank you? Are you leaving now? I just – "

"Do you want me to leave?" He grasped her chin gently and raised her face to his.

"No. I want you to stay the night with me," she whispered.

"Then I will." He kissed the tip of her nose. "Why don't we go downstairs and I'll cook you my world-famous French toast?"

"All right." She gave him a shy smile and he couldn't resist kissing her sweet mouth.

"Good." He pulled on his pants but didn't bother with his shirt as she watched from the doorway. His gaze fell on the yellow nightie still draped across the end of the bed and he picked it up.

"Will you wear this, Jules?"

She clutched the neckline of her robe for a moment and then nodded. "Yes."

He watched, his gaze roaming hungrily over her naked body as she shed her robe and quickly pulled the nightgown over her head. The flimsy material clung to her breasts and stopped at the middle of her thighs. He stared at the dark shadow between her thighs, just barely visible through the thin material. She blushed furiously and a small smile of satisfaction crossed his lips when she stopped herself from crossing her arms over her breasts.

"You look beautiful, Jules."

"Thank you," she replied softly.

"I'll meet you downstairs. I just need to use the bathroom."

She nodded and left the bedroom. He quickly used the washroom before fishing his phone out of his suit jacket. He sent a short text to Cal and shut the phone off before his brother could reply. He took a condom from the bedside table and slipped it into his pocket before leaving the room.

* * *

"Do you like to cook?"

He shrugged as he flipped the bread in the pan. "I don't hate it. A few years ago, after living on canned soup and frozen dinners for way too long, I had my mom teach me a bunch of stuff about cooking. She got a kick out of that. When we were younger, she tried to teach me and my siblings how to cook but my sister was the only one who actually paid any attention."

"Are you close to your siblings?" Julie asked.

He nodded. "I'm probably closest to my brother but I get along with my sister. She's a few years younger than us so we gave her some grief as kids but she's forgiven us for all the teasing."

"I always wanted a sister. Someone I could share clothes and make-up and secrets with," Julie said.

"Why didn't your dad remarry?"

She shrugged. "I don't know."

She rubbed her hand across the smooth surface of the kitchen table. Her father had never brought a woman home to meet her. She suspected that he was dating, occasionally he would go out at night and come home smelling of perfume, but over the years even that dwindled to a stop.

Court slid a piece of French toast on to the plate in front of her before placing one on his own. Behind him, two more pieces sizzled in the pan and he handed her the syrup. "Eat up."

She dug into the French toast as her belly rumbled. It was delicious and she grinned at him. "It's really good."

"Thanks." He ate his quickly and flipped the other pieces as she savoured each bite. She shook her head when he brought the second piece to her.

"I'd better not."

He frowned. "One piece of French toast isn't enough for dinner, Jules."

"It's delicious, really it is, but it's pretty high in calories so – "

He slid the piece onto her plate. "You'll need the energy. Trust me, darlin'."

She blushed at the implication and his grin widened as he sat down. "God, I really do love the way you blush."

She rolled her eyes as she poured syrup onto the toast. "It's embarrassing."

"It's adorable," he countered.

They ate silently for a few moments before he stared thoughtfully at her. "So, now that your dad is gone are you going to go back to school to be an architect?"

"God, no. I'm too old for that now."

"No you're not. People go back to school at any age. If it's what you've always wanted to do, why not go for it?"

"I – I hadn't really thought about it, to be honest."

He finished his food and she stood and took their plates as he leaned back in his chair. "You should think about it."

"Maybe I will." She quickly rinsed their plates before bending and placing them in the dishwasher. He stared at her ass. The nightgown barely covered it when she bent and as she straightened, he reached out and stroked one firm cheek.

She jumped and peered wide-eyed over her shoulder at him as he continued to caress her ass. He slid his hand under her nightgown and cupped and massaged her bare ass before he pushed his chair back and patted his lap.

"Come here, Jules."

She swallowed nervously before approaching him. He shook his head when she went to sit down. "No, straddle me."

"I – I'm not wearing underwear." His touch and the way he was looking at her had been enough to bring on an embarrassing amount of wetness between her thighs and he was bound to notice when she dripped all over his damn pants.

Her face flamed and she bit at her bottom lip. Court was going to think she was some kind of freak. Normal women didn't get this wet from having their ass groped, did they?

"I'm aware of that." There was amusement in his voice and she resisted when he tugged lightly on her hand.

"I – I don't want to ruin your pants," she whispered.

He cocked his head at her. "Why would you ruin my pants?"

"Because I'm – I'm..."

She couldn't say it. Not in this brightly-lit kitchen. Not when she was feeling exposed and needy and barely able to stop from drooling with lust all over his broad, naked chest.

His eyes suddenly darkened with need as understanding washed over him and she felt an answering call of desire deep in her pelvis. Her pussy throbbed and her nipples hardened as he stood. He reached into his pocket and placed a condom on the table before placing one arm around her. His hand pressed firmly in the small of her back and she couldn't stop her soft moan when she felt his erection press against her belly.

"Are you wet for me, Julie?" He rubbed her back with one big hand.

"Court, I – "

"Are you?" His hand moved to her ass and he squeezed it firmly.

She moaned, her head falling back when he lowered his mouth to her throat. He nipped it and then licked the spot soothingly.

"Is your pussy wet?" He murmured.

"Yes," she whispered.

"Say it."

"I can't."

"Yes, you can." He bit her throat again and she jerked against him.

"My pussy is wet for you." She could hear the need in her voice.

"Spread your legs, Jules." He waited patiently until she shifted her thighs apart.

He slipped his hand under her nightgown and cupped her pussy. She cried out when his fingers touched her slick flesh and was helpless to stop the arch of her back.

"So wet," he groaned as she made a soft mewl of need.

"I love how needy you are for my cock," he growled into her ear as his fingers rubbed at her swollen clit.

She shuddered with desire and rubbed herself against his hand as he bit at her earlobe. She wondered if all men were like this. If they could go from such sweetness to dark desire in a heartbeat the way that Court did. His words were turning her on almost as much as his hand between her thighs. Did other women enjoy dirty talk? Did he think it strange that she liked hearing him say pussy and cock? She had no idea and didn't have the courage to ask.

He moved his hand away and she cried out with disappointment. He sucked on her lower lip as his hand moved to the button of his pants. He undid them quickly and pushed them down his hips until they pooled at his feet.

He sat naked on the chair before patting his lap again. "Problem solved, Jules."

She stared at his cock as he rolled the condom onto it. It was standing up proudly from the nest of dark hair that surrounded it and she felt a curious sense of pride.

I did that to him, she thought and another odd tickle of pride went through her.

"Julie." His low voice had her raising her glance to him.

"Straddle me, now."

His softly-worded demand made her shudder all over and she quickly straddled him. His cock brushed against her pussy and she arched her hips, trying to take him inside of her.

"Not yet," he growled again and she gave him a look of frustration.

"I want you." She'd never heard her voice like that before – breathless and almost on the verge of an embarrassing whine.

"I know," he said and petted her back soothingly. "Soon."

He pulled off her nightgown and dropped it to the floor. She felt a moment of embarrassment as he gazed at her naked body in the bright, unforgiving lights of the kitchen but it disappeared quickly when he cupped one heavy breast and lifted it to his hot, wet mouth. He sucked firmly on her nipple before pulling lightly on it with his teeth. She arched her back, her hands clutching at his thick hair as he moved back and forth between her breasts. His mouth was driving her crazy. The way he used his lips and teeth and tongue to drive her into a frenzy of need as he pulled and sucked and licked at her swollen, throbbing nipples made her want to thrust herself on to his cock.

She reached between them and grabbed his cock. She rubbed it shamelessly against her clit, her need driving her embarrassment and uncertainty from her, as she gasped and moaned. He let her use his cock as he continued to suck and bite at her nipples, and she was on the verge of an orgasm when he reached between them and pulled her hand away.

"No!" She cried out with frustration and tried to yank her hand free.

He kissed her deeply on the mouth, shoving his tongue between her lips and coaxing her tongue into his. He sucked hard on her tongue as he lifted her and guided his cock into her wet, tight core.

She tore her mouth free, her fingers digging into his back as she panted harshly. "Oh God!" She stretched around his hardness, her walls clinging tightly to his cock as he thrust deeply into her. She clung to his shoulders, her shyness forgotten completely, as she bounced on his cock. He groaned and slid in and out of her as she drove her body up and down on his.

He reached between them and rubbed her clit with the ball of his thumb. She contracted tightly around him as she screamed hoarsely and he buried his face in the curve of her neck. Her pussy tightened and released him in a glorious rhythm as she came and he gave in to the driving need to come and thrust one final time into her.

She shook and moaned loudly as he kissed her neck repeatedly before she collapsed against him. He stroked her warm back and held her tightly as she burrowed into him and wrapped her arms around his shoulders.

After a few minutes, she raised her head and stared at him. "Wow."

He hugged her tightly. "Wow doesn't even begin to describe it, darlin'."

She kissed his neck tentatively and he stared blankly at the kitchen wall as he shifted her closer. He was already dreading leaving her tomorrow and he sighed quietly. What had he gotten himself into?

Chapter 8

Julie stared at the phone in her hand before pacing back and forth in her bedroom. Court had left yesterday morning and she had resigned herself to never seeing him again. She had walked him to the door and then nervously thanked him.

"It was my pleasure, Jules," he had whispered before kissing her and leaving.

She had spent the day in a funk, ignoring Mary's texts and constantly reminding herself that Court had only been doing what she had paid him to do. It didn't matter that just before he showered and left, he had made love to her with such sweetness that she'd had to hold back tears.

She had dreamed about him last night. Dreamed he was back in her bed and his hard hands and hot mouth were making her nerve endings sing with anticipation. She had woken from her dream, her body sweating and her pussy aching, and stared blankly at the ceiling until the sun crept across the horizon.

Now, she stared again at her cell phone.

Call, her mind whispered. *There's nothing wrong with calling for another date with Court. You wanted him to teach you how to please a man in bed and do you really think one night is enough to teach you what to do? Besides, he spent the night pleasuring you, remember? You didn't even go down on him for God's sake! Do you really want to go out and find a boyfriend when you don't even know how to perform oral sex? Call and make another date with Court. He'll be happy to let you practice on him.*

Her fingers trembling, Julie called the number.

"Vanessa's Escort Agency. How may I help you?" Meagan's now-familiar voice answered after the first ring.

"Um, hi Meagan. It's uh, Julie Winslow calling?"

"Hello Julie. How are you?" Meagan said warmly.

"I'm uh, I'm good, thanks. I was just calling because I wanted to arrange another um, date with Cou – uh, Cal?" Julie said nervously.

"Of course!"

She could hear the clicking of Meagan's nails against the keyboard and she took a deep breath.

"What night were you looking for, Julie?"

"Tonight, please," she replied.

"Oh, I'm sorry. Cal is already booked tonight and tomorrow night. I could book you for Friday though."

Julie, her ears ringing and her heart thudding painfully in her chest, tried desperately to squeak out a reply.

"Hello? Julie, are you there?"

"Yes," she gasped out. "I'm sorry. I uh, Friday night won't work for me."

"What about Saturday? He's available Saturday," Meagan said cheerfully.

"Oh, I um, I'll have to check my schedule. Can I call you back?" Julie whispered.

"Of course. Talk to you soon, Julie."

Julie hit the end button and then threw her cell phone on the bed. She was dismayed to realize that tears were starting to flow down her cheeks and she wiped them away hurriedly as she sank to the floor of her bedroom. She buried her face in her hands. Court was going out tonight with a woman who had paid him just like she had. He would be taking her to bed and giving her the same pleasure that he –

A hiccupping sob escaped her throat and this time she let the hot tears course down her cheeks. She was an idiot. Court was paid to have sex with women. Just because he was kind and sweet and made her first time more wonderful than she could ever have imagined, it didn't mean he cared for her. He had been paid to take her virginity and he had done it. She was crazy if she thought they could have some kind of relationship.

* * *

Three hours later when Mary came storming into the house, Julie was sitting on the couch in the living room, wrapped in a blanket and eating ice cream.

"Jesus, Julie!" She gave her an angry look. "You scared the hell out of me!"

"What are you talking about, Mare?" Julie asked wearily before eating another spoonful of ice cream.

"You haven't responded to any of my texts! I thought that Court guy had tied you up in your basement and was torturing you!" She snapped.

Julie shook her head. "I'm fine."

Mary set her jacket on the chair and dropped on to the couch next to her. She took a good look at Julie's swollen eyelids and pale face. "What happened? Did he hurt you? I'll kill the son of a bitch if he did."

"He didn't hurt me, Mary." Julie stirred her melting ice cream before setting it on the coffee table. "I had a good time."

"Did you sleep with him?"

Julie nodded and wrapped the blanket more firmly around her.

Mary touched her shoulder hesitantly. "Jules, sometimes the first time isn't all that spectacular, you know? It can be weird and awkward and painful. It doesn't mean that – "

"It was good," Julie interrupted.

"What does that mean?" Mary asked.

"It means that it was good," Julie said grumpily. "He made it nice."

"Nice?" Mary raised her eyebrow at her. "Jules, tell me what really happened "

Julie sighed with irritation. "What do you want me to say, Mary? That it was magical and special and the most amazing night of my life? It was! Court made me feel gorgeous and wanted and I had so many orgasms, I lost count! There! Are you happy now?"

She waited for Mary to get angry at her, to tell her to kiss her ass and storm out, and she could feel the tears threatening again when Mary scooted closer and put her arm around her. She hugged Julie tightly and kissed the top of her head when Julie rested her cheek against her shoulder.

"Then why are you sad? Why are you sitting in your dark house, wrapped in a blanket and eating ice cream?"

Julie shrugged. "I don't know. I just – I guess I thought maybe Court felt something for me."

Mary frowned. "Julie, he was being paid to – "

"I know!" Julie nearly shouted. "I'm a silly little girl who thought a man paid to deflower me, wanted something more!"

Mary winced and held her more tightly. "I'm so sorry, Jules. This is all my fault."

"It isn't, Mary. It was a good idea and I'll get over it. I will. It was the right thing to do and I'm happy I did it."

"Are you?" Mary gave her a searching look.

"Yes," Julie said firmly. She wasn't lying. Despite everything, she couldn't regret giving Court her virginity. She might have paid him to do it but for that brief time, he had made her forget that he was only doing a job. She would always be grateful to him.

"I just need some time," she repeated herself.

"No. What you need is a distraction," Mary said firmly. "We're going out Friday night."

"What? No, I can't." Julie gave her a horrified look.

"You can and you will," Mary replied. "You paid a man to take your virginity so you didn't have to worry about it. Now it's time to find your happily ever after."

"Mary – "

Mary shook her head. "No, Jules. I'm not letting you back out of the plan. You want to find someone, don't you? Well, you're not going to find them sitting in the dark and eating ice cream. We're going out Friday night and that's final."

* * *

"What the hell is wrong with you, man?"

Court glared at his best friend. "Nothing's wrong with me, Mark."

"Bullshit." Mark took a sip of his beer and stretched his jean-clad legs out under the table. "You've been moping around for the last three days at work and you tore a strip off of Jim earlier."

"Nothing's wrong." Court took his own swallow of beer and stared moodily around the bar. He was already regretting letting Mark drag him out to this meat market after work. He hadn't wanted to go but he hadn't wanted to go back to his empty apartment either. He had done nothing but think about Julie all week and he had texted Cal twice to find out if she had set up another date.

She hadn't and he was more hurt by that then he had any right to be. Julie had made it clear what she was looking for and besides, what did he think was going to happen between them? She thought he was an escort for God's sake.

He sighed and wiped at a smear of dirt on his jeans. They had worked late, working straight through dinner and into the night, and they had come straight from the construction site to the bar. He was feeling remarkably out of place. He had thought they would hit their usual pub, it was full of blue-collar workers like himself, and he felt awkward and out of place in this dark and noisy club.

"Why the hell did you drag me here anyway?" He asked irritably. "What's wrong with Flannigan's?"

Mark rolled his eyes. "In case you haven't noticed, the ratio of women to men in Flannigan's is horrendous. This place has got plenty of eye candy."

He eyed the skimpily-dressed women sauntering past their table and tipped his beer to them. They looked both him and Court up and down, and Court felt his face burn when one of them whispered to the others and the lot of them broke into that high-pitched giggling that made his ears bleed.

"We don't belong here, Mark," he said through gritted teeth. "One, the women here are all barely over eighteen and two, they don't want guys like us. They want pretty boys who can buy them whatever they want and take them out on daddy's goddamn sailboat."

Mark scoffed loudly. "Whatever, man. The ladies in this place love men like us. They think they want those boys who wouldn't know a goddamn hammer from a screwdriver but I guarantee you that by the end of the night, they'll be all over us."

"Yeah, great," Court muttered.

"Seriously, man." Mark gave him an irritated look. "What the fuck is going on with you? It's about time you got over that bitch Janine and got yourself some young, hot tail. Christ, you're the only guy I know who would turn down a woman's invitation for a night of hot, meaningless sex."

"Yes, because hot, meaningless sex solves everyone's problems," Court responded dryly.

"Hey, don't knock it until you've tried it." Mark shrugged and took another drink of beer. "Last week I met up with this smoking hot chick. She took me back to her place and Christ on a pony could that girl suck. She was like a goddamn Hoover. I've never had so – "

He stopped as Court cursed loudly. The crowd of people had thinned a bit and Mark followed his gaze to the woman perched nervously on a bar stool at one of the small tables scattered throughout the room. She was dressed in jeans and a soft pink blouse and she was smiling faintly at the blond man leaning casually against the table.

"She ain't half-bad," Mark said appraisingly. "A little chubby but those tits are – "

"Shut up, Mark," Court growled.

Mark shook his head. "You know her?"

"Yes," Court bit out. His hand tightened on his beer bottle when the blond man reached out and brushed the woman's dark hair back from her face.

"You should introduce me to her friend. You know I like the reds." Mark was gazing appreciatively at the slender redhead sitting next to the woman. She had her own admirer and she was talking animatedly to him as the dark-haired woman took a quick sip of her drink.

"I bet that redhead is dynamite in the sack. They always are. I think it's the red hair, man. It makes them – "

Mark blinked in surprise. He was talking to thin air. Court had stood and was pushing his way through the crowd of people between them and the women. Mark grabbed his beer and followed.

"So, Julie. Tell me what you like to do for fun." The blond man, Julie thought his name was Jake or maybe it was Hank, it was nearly impossible to hear over the loud beat of music blaring from the dance floor, stroked her arm lightly.

"Oh, you know, the usual," she replied.

He leaned a little closer, his breath stirring her hair, and she tried not to wince. He smelled like beer and pot and although he was handsome enough, she had a feeling he wasn't a day over twenty-one.

"Listen, what do you say we get out of here?" Jake/Hank said into her ear. "My apartment isn't far from here. We can put up our feet, listen to some music and get to know each other a little better."

He placed his hand on her waist and she shoved his hand away when his fingers tried to caress the underside of her breast.

"I literally just met you ten minutes ago." She gave him a look of exasperation.

He shrugged and gave her what he probably thought was a panty-melting smile. "I know, baby. I also know what you older ladies are looking for and I'm more than happy to give it to you."

She gaped at him. "Are you kidding me?"

He shrugged again. "Not at all, baby. Why don't you let me show you a good time?"

He was reaching out to caress her arm again when a hand grabbed his upper arm and jerked him away.

"What the fuck, man?" He glared at the large man in the dirty t-shirt. "What the fuck is your problem?"

"Court!" Julie stared in surprise at Court. He was dressed in jeans and a white t-shirt. The shirt had smears of dirt on it and she could see dust and dirt in the creases of his thick neck. He held his hand out to her.

"C'mon, Jules."

She took his hand, sliding off the barstool as Mary grabbed at her arm.

"Julie? Where are you going?"

Julie glanced at Court as he linked his fingers with hers. The music changed, became a slow, seductive beat, and she licked her lips nervously as he looked her up and down.

"Buddy, I don't know who the hell you think you are but I'm with the lady so why don't you get lost." The blond man put his hand on Court's arm.

Court glanced down at the man. "Unless you want to spend the night in the emergency room with a broken hand, you'd be wise to get lost, *kid,*" he said dismissively.

The blond man dropped his arm and took a step back. "Forget it. She ain't worth it."

He nodded to his friend and the two of them walked away as Mark laughed loudly and plopped down on the bar stool next to Mary.

"Court?" Julie cleared her throat nervously and he tightened his hand around hers.

"Let's dance, Jules."

He led her toward the dance floor as Mark winked at Mary. "Hello, gorgeous. Can I buy you a drink?"

"What – what are you doing here?" Julie squeaked out as Court pulled her into his arms. He swayed in time with the music as she tried to ignore the butterflies that were starting in her stomach.

"What are *you* doing here? This place is nothing but a meat market, Jules." He glared at her.

She bit at her bottom lip and he almost groaned with need. He wanted to kiss her, wanted to touch her warm skin, hell he wanted to carry her off to a dark corner somewhere and fuck her senseless. He casually moved his pelvis away from her as his cock hardened in his jeans.

"I – I just wanted to have a night out," she said softly. "Maybe meet someone."

"At this place?" He glared again at her. "The men that come here are only interested in one thing, Julie."

"Is that why you're here?" She gave him a defiant look.

"Mark dragged me here," he muttered. "I didn't want to go but thank God I did. Who knows what would have happened to you if I hadn't shown up."

She stiffened in his arms. "I can take care of myself, Court. I don't need you babysitting me."

He scowled at her. "You're naïve and sweet. You're like candy to these assholes."

She didn't reply and he grunted angrily. "Is that what you want, Julie? A quick bang with an idiot like the blond Boy-Wonder back there?"

"What's wrong with that?" She snapped. "I'm a grown woman, I can do whatever I want. If I want to - to have meaningless sex with some random stranger at a bar, I will."

His nostrils flared angrily and she gave him another look of defiance as he pulled her tightly against his body. He lowered his mouth to her ear as he ground his erection against her.

"None of these silly, little boys can please you the way I can, darlin'. I guarantee you that not one of them will make your pussy as wet as I do. Not one of them will make you scream. Do you remember how good it felt when I fucked you? I remember. I remember how wet and hot and tight you were. I remember how you begged for my cock. Do you believe any of those boys could make you beg the way that I do?"

He cupped the back of her head and wound his fingers through her thick dark hair. They had slowed to a near stop. He ignored the other couples on the dance floor who were bumping lightly against them as they moved past.

"Do you, Jules?" His hand tightened in her hair and she gave a soft moan of need when he lowered his head and sucked on her upper lip.

"No," she whispered.

"That's right, darlin'." He moved his hand to her ass and squeezed it as he flicked his tongue along the shell of her ear.

"Your pussy was made for my cock and only mine," he whispered.

Julie moaned again. Her entire body was filled with a lust so deep she felt like her skin was on fire. His coarse words, the way he acted like she belonged to him, made her feel delirious with desire.

"Court, please," she whispered.

He sucked on her earlobe as she clutched at his back. His erection was hot and throbbing against her and despite being surrounded by a sea of people, she could only see and hear and feel him.

"Have you missed me, Jules?" He breathed into her ear. "Have you missed fucking me?"

"Yes," she answered immediately.

He chuckled, a warm sound that vibrated against her breasts, and she flushed as he squeezed her ass again. "You've got an itch that needs scratching. Don't you, darlin'?"

She nodded again and he nipped her earlobe. "You should have called me. I know what you need."

She froze against him and he leaned back. "Jules? What's wrong?"

"I did call," she said softly. "You were all booked up."

His stomach dropped at the look on her face and he could feel panic starting when she tried to pull away. "I should go, Court."

He held her more tightly, wrapping his arms around her waist as she stood tensely against him. "I'm sorry, Jules."

She shrugged. "Don't be. It's your job."

He didn't respond and she couldn't keep the bitterness from her voice. "You're very popular. Fully booked this week. I guess I know why."

He said the only thing he could think of. "I didn't sleep with any of them, Julie."

She twitched in his arms and looked up at him. "What?"

"I didn't sleep with them. I swear to you."

"Why not? Isn't that what they pay you for?"

"Not always." He gave her a pleading look. "Do you believe me?"

She nodded and he breathed a sigh of relief. They resumed swaying to the music as she buried her face in his throat. "What do we do now?"

He hugged her tightly. "Spend the night with me."

She stared up at him. "Court, that isn't a good idea. We can't – "

"Just one more night, Jules." He knew he was begging like a pathetic teenage boy but he didn't care. "No escort agency, no money or time limits. Just us making each other feel good. I need you."

She hesitated and his arms tightened almost painfully around her. "A-all right."

He released his breath in a harsh rush and kissed her hard on the mouth. "Let's go."

"I need to talk to Mary first," she said breathlessly.

He nodded and led her back to the table. Mary was staring amused at Mark who was waving his hands as he talked loudly.

"Mary? I'm leaving. Will you be okay?" Julie asked.

Mary frowned and slid off the barstool. She took Julie's arm and pulled her a short distance away. "What are you doing, Julie? You don't need to pay him for a damn date. There are plenty of guys in here who – "

"I'm not paying him," Julie interrupted. "Listen, I need to go. Will you be okay or do you want us to drop you off at home?"

"Honey, I don't think – "

"Stop it, Mary," Julie said harshly. "I'm a grown woman and I know what I'm doing." Her gaze drifted back to Court. He was staring at her and her pussy tingled with anticipation at his look of dark desire.

"Do you?" Mary said softly.

"Yes." Julie nodded impatiently as she glanced again at Court. "Please, I'm asking you to trust me."

"Fine," Mary sighed. "Go on then."

"Do you need a ride home first?"

Mary shook her head. "Nope. Believe it or not I'm actually enjoying Mark's company. I'm going to stick around and see where it leads."

"Okay." Julie was already drifting away and Mary caught her arm.

"Be careful, Julie. Don't give your heart to him, okay?"

"I won't," she lied.

Chapter 9

"Sit beside me." Court patted the seat beside him and Julie slid to the middle as he started the truck and drove out of the parking lot.

He put his hand on her thigh and rubbed it as he drove down the dark, empty streets. When his hand slid between her thighs and cupped her firmly through her jeans she inhaled sharply and grabbed his arm.

"Court," she moaned.

"Yes, Jules?" He rubbed his callused fingers over her and she arched her hips into his hand.

"That feels so good."

He smiled. "Undo your jeans."

She hesitated and he rubbed her again. "Undo them."

Her fingers shaking, she unbuttoned and unzipped her jeans and cried out with pleasure when he pushed his hand past her underwear and slid two fingers deep inside of her. She wiggled against his hand and he groaned appreciatively.

"Fuck. You're so goddamn tight, Jules."

He moved his fingers in and out of her as she closed her eyes and thrust her pelvis against him. He ground the heel of his hand against her clit, and she moaned loudly as she spread her legs wide.

"That's right, darlin'," he murmured. "Keep them wide open for me."

She clutched compulsively at his arm as he moved his fingers rapidly back and forth. "Do you like that, Jules?"

"Yes, oh yes," she muttered.

She panted and thrust against his hand as he continued to drive. Lust was growing inside of her, making her insides burn, and he gave another soft murmur of approval when her muscles clenched around his fingers.

When he curled his fingers inside of her and the pads of his callused fingers rubbed against the rough patch of skin on the front wall of her pussy, she nearly slid off the seat.

"Oh my God! Court!" She cried out loudly and he grinned at her.

"Should I do that again, Jules?"

"Yes! Please!" She moaned.

"Whatever you want, darlin'," he whispered before rubbing again.

Her back arched and her ass came up off the seat as her pussy tightened exquisitely around his fingers. She came loudly, her hoarse voice filling the cab of the truck, as she writhed and squirmed on his fingers. She collapsed against the seat, her heart beating like a drum in her chest, as he pulled his hand free and sucked on one finger.

"Delicious," he murmured, sending another twinge of desire through her belly.

She realized he had shut off the truck and she stared dazedly at her dark house. "We're home?"

"Yes." He opened the door and slid out of the truck, holding out his hand. "Let's go, Jules. Unless you want me to fuck you in your front yard."

She took his hand and followed him to the front door. Her hands were shaking so badly she could barely hold her keys and with a soft grunt of impatience, he took them from her and unlocked the door. He pushed her inside and slammed the door shut behind them before pushing her up against the wall.

He kissed her hard on the mouth, her insides turning to jelly, as he pushed his tongue past her parted lips and explored her warm mouth. He cupped her breasts, rubbing his thumbs over her nipples before he tore open the front of her blouse. Buttons went flying as he yanked down the cups of her bra and bent his head to her breasts. He latched on to one stiff nipple, his lips worrying it into an almost painful hardness as she clutched at his head and moaned loudly.

Without speaking he backed away from her and she gave him a look of confusion. "Court, what's wrong?"

"Nothing." He took her hand and moved swiftly through the dark house. "I'm going to explode if I don't fuck you, Julie."

They climbed the staircase and hurried into her bedroom. She had barely stepped into the room before he was on her. His hands were everywhere, warm and hard and kneading her pale flesh as he pulled her shirt from her body and quickly unhooked her bra.

She yanked at his t-shirt, pulling it over his head, as he shoved her jeans and her underwear to her feet. She stumbled and nearly fell and, with another grunt of impatience, he lifted her out of the confining fabric and carried her to the bed.

He kissed her again before setting her down on the bed. "Get on your hands and knees, Jules."

She swallowed nervously but obeyed his command as he pulled a condom from his pocket and shoved his jeans and boxers down his legs. She heard the rustle of the foil wrapper and then his hands were on her hips and he was pulling her to the edge of the bed.

He stepped between her legs, his rough hair-covered thighs pushing hers apart, and she moaned when his cock slipped across her wetness. He took her hand and pushed it between her thighs. "Spread yourself open for me."

Her fingers trembling, she pushed apart the lips of her pussy. He could see her clit, swollen and wet and he rubbed the head of his cock against it. She made a soft, gasping noise of pleasure and he growled in response before guiding his cock to her wet opening. He pushed the head in, his stomach tightening with pleasure as he watched the lips of her pussy sliding down his cock. He pushed again, her slick heat welcoming him as he slid into her until his pelvis was snug against her ass.

He leaned over her and kissed her bare back before gathering her long dark hair into his hand. He tugged lightly until she raised her head and he cupped her throat gently as he kissed her cheek.

"Your pussy was made for my cock," he repeated his words from the bar and she shuddered around him, her pussy squeezing him until he groaned.

"Only mine. Do you understand, Jules?"

"Yes. Only yours," she gasped. "Please, Court. I need you."

"I need you too, darlin'." He kissed her cheek again before beginning to fuck her. She moaned and thrust back against him, meeting each of his hard strokes. He dropped his hands to her hips, holding her tightly as he plunged in and out of her.

They moved against each other, their bodies slapping together in a quick rhythm as he drove harder and deeper into her. His need was making him rough, and he tried to slow down before he hurt her but she was making soft mewls of pleasure that were driving his need higher. He reached under her and cupped her breasts, pulling roughly on her nipples, and she screamed his name as she came helplessly around his thick cock.

His breath coming in harsh, hot pants, he drove in and out of her, his hands tightening on her wide hips as he shoved in to the hilt and his orgasm roared through him. He collapsed against her, driving her into the mattress and placed hard, frantic kisses against her bare back before rolling off of her. She turned on her side and curled up against him, staring wide-eyed at him, as she put her arm around his waist.

"Did I hurt you?" He said hoarsely.

She shook her head. "God, no. That was – it was…"

She trailed off and he grinned down at her. "I know exactly what you mean."

* * *

"That's right, darlin'," Court murmured. "Keep doing that." He stroked Julie's wet hair as he stared down at her.

"You look so pretty with your lips wrapped around my cock, Jules." He stroked her hair again before sliding his cock deeper into her mouth.

She stared up at him as she sucked hard on his cock and he groaned loudly. The hot water of the shower rained down on his back and he pulled free of her hot, wet mouth as she licked her swollen lips.

She gave him a look of desperate need before attacking his cock again. She licked him eagerly, swirling her tongue around the tip, and his hands tightened in her hair as she took his cock deep into her mouth. She bobbed her head back and forth, licking along his cock as she sucked, and he closed his eyes and tilted his head back. He desperately wanted to come in her mouth but he forced himself to hold back. He knew he was clean but he didn't want Julie to have any worries so with another loud groan, he pulled free of her mouth and yanked her to her feet.

"Did I do something wrong, Court?" She asked worriedly.

"Christ, no." He sucked on her swollen, bottom lip. "Not at all, darlin'. It feels amazing."

She reached down and gripped him with her hand, stroking back and forth as his hips thrust against her. "Then why did you stop me?"

He smiled at her and cupped her naked, wet breast. "I think it's time I returned the favor, don't you?"

She inhaled sharply and gave him a shy look. "I'd like that."

"Me too." He shut off the shower and opened the door. They towelled off quickly and he led her back into her bedroom.

"Lie down, Julie."

It was Saturday and the late afternoon sun shone through her window onto her bed. She lay down in the warm patch of sunlight and he lay down next to her. He cupped her breast and kissed her warm mouth before dipping his head to suck on her nipple.

"Oh, Court," she moaned softly as he moved down her body, licking and sucking on her warm, pale flesh as she shifted restlessly beneath him.

He pushed her thighs open and knelt between her legs before he traced her navel with his tongue. She shivered with delight and he smiled up at her before kissing her round belly. "Ready, Jules?"

"Yes," she moaned softly and he slid further down until his mouth was directly above her pussy. He kissed her soft curls as he slid his hands under her and cupped her full ass. She was nervous, he could tell by the tenseness of her thighs and the way she stared wide-eyed at the ceiling, and he kissed her soft curls again.

"Relax, Jules."

"I am," she lied.

He grinned. "You aren't. Spread your legs for me, darlin'."

"Court, I – "

She was staring anxiously at him and he gave her a reassuring smile.

"Relax your legs. Let me make you feel good."

She relaxed her legs and he stared at her exposed, glistening sex. "Wider, darlin'."

She widened her legs and he licked his lips when he saw her clit. He dipped his head and licked it delicately. She gasped and jerked against the bed, her thighs closing against his head before she let them fall wide open.

"That's my good girl," he whispered. He licked her clit repeatedly, stroking it with wide, flat strokes of his tongue before he dipped into her wet opening.

She was moaning and panting above him, her hands digging into the sheets on the bed and he grinned again before sucking her clit into his mouth.

"Court!" She cried his name and her hands reached for his head. She clutched it tightly, pushing him against her as she thrust her hips at his face.

He pressed down on her hips, holding her steady against the bed as he licked and sucked at her clit. It swelled in his mouth and he rubbed it with his tongue as she moaned loudly and arched up off the bed.

"That's right, darlin'," he murmured. "Let me hear how much you need me."

She thrust against him again and with a loud cry came wildly against his mouth, her thighs tightening around his head as her orgasm shook her entire body. He lapped at her, tasting her sweetness as she collapsed against the bed. He sat up and quickly put a condom on before moving up her body. He entered her with one hard thrust and cupped her head.

"Look at me, Jules."

Her eyes fluttered open and she stared hazily at him as he tugged on her thigh. "Wrap your legs around me."

She did as he asked, hooking her feet into the small of his back as he plunged in and out of her.

"You tasted so sweet, Jules. I could eat your pussy for hours."

She groaned in reply, her legs and pussy tightening around him, and he responded by thrusting more roughly into her.

"Oh Court," she moaned softly.

"Jules," he whispered before he buried his face in her throat and lost himself in the sweet warmth of her body.

* * *

"Thank you, Court. I had a really great time this weekend," Julie said quietly.

He stood in the hallway, his hand on the front door, and stared gravely at her. It was Sunday evening, just after dinner, and it was ridiculous how badly he wanted to stay with her. He made a sudden decision.

"Give me your phone, Jules."

Giving him a questioning look, she handed it over and he quickly added his name and number to her phone. "This is my cell number. Call me, okay?"

She hesitated and his stomach dropped. "If you don't want to I'll understand, but just think about it. Will you?"

She nodded and he kissed her lightly on the mouth. "Bye, Jules."

"Bye, Court." She smiled at him but as she closed the door, he had a terrible feeling that he'd never hear from her again.

Chapter 10

Julie sipped at her tea and stared out the kitchen window. It was Monday evening and she had spent the entire day wandering around her house and staring at her phone. She had come close to texting Court numerous times but had stopped herself.

You can't have a relationship with him. He's an escort. He sleeps with women for money. Do you really think you can have a relationship with a guy who sleeps with other women?

She sighed and stared morosely out the window. She was being a hypocrite. It was fine for her to hire Court to sleep with her but not fine for him to do the same for other women? She took another sip of tea. She didn't want to share him – it was that simple. If that made her a horrible person, so be it.

She reached for her phone and scrolled to Court's number. Her finger hovered over the delete button before she put her phone down and rubbed her forehead wearily. If she knew she couldn't have a relationship with him, why couldn't she delete his number? She stared at her phone and reached again for it. She needed to talk to Mary.

* * *

Court checked his cell phone as he opened the door to his apartment. He had checked it compulsively all day and he ignored the wave of disappointment that went through him.

It's only been a day, Court. Just relax. She'll call.

He blew out his breath and tossed his keys on the side table before going to the kitchen.

"Where have you been?"

He jumped and flicked on the light. Cal was sitting at the table and he stared at Court as he bit at his nails.

"Christ, Cal! You scared the hell out of me! Why are you sitting here in the dark?"

"Where have you been, Court?"

"I've been at work. Where do you think I've been?" He frowned as he opened the fridge and pulled out a beer.

"Where were you on the weekend? I came by Saturday and Sunday," Cal said accusingly.

"I was with a friend."

"Who?"

"Why all the questions?" Court scowled at him.

"Why are you avoiding my question?"

"I'm not."

"You are. Who have you been with?"

Court sighed. "Julie, all right? I was with Julie."

"Jesus Christ, Court!" Cal jumped up and paced nervously through the kitchen. "What the hell are you doing?"

"Cal, I – "

"You can't see a client outside of working hours. I told you that!"

"She's not just a goddamn client, Cal! You have no idea what she's like. She's sweet and kind and I like her. Do you hear me? I like her. I'm going to tell her the truth."

"You like her?" Cal shook his head in disbelief. "Court, this is crazy. You're going to get me fired. You can't tell her the truth!"

"I can and I will," he said firmly.

"And what do you think she'll say when she finds out you've been lying to her? Do you think she'll just forgive you and tell you everything's fine?" Cal asked.

"I'm willing to take that chance."

"Is it because she's a goddamn millionaire?"

"How do you know that?"

Cal sighed. "Meagan told me that Julie had called last week and wanted to book me for another appointment. I wondered how she could afford me so I did some research. It didn't take long to figure out who she was."

"It has nothing to do with her money, Cal," Court said tightly.

"Of course it doesn't." Cal laughed bitterly. "You've never cared about money. You've never had to."

"What's going on with you, Cal?" Court asked suddenly. "There's something wrong, I know there is."

"I'm fine." Cal rubbed his hand through his hair. "It's just – I..."

"What?"

"Never mind. It doesn't matter." He stared silently at Court for a moment. "Listen, I gotta go. I'll talk to you later, okay?"

"Cal, wait. Tell me what's going on? Does it have something to do with that investment thing? Did you get turned down?" Court followed him out of the kitchen and down the hallway.

Cal shook his head. "It didn't work out. I gotta go, Court."

He slipped out of the apartment before Court could reply.

* * *

"Mary? Are you busy?" Julie could hardly hear Mary's reply over the loud music blaring through her cell phone.

"Hold on, Jules!" Mary shouted.

The music was turned down and she heard Mary giggle brightly before she came back on the phone. She sounded slightly out of breath and Julie frowned.

"Mary? Where are you?"

"I'm um, well, I'm with Mark."

"Mark?"

"From the bar. Court's friend."

"Really?" Julie dropped into a kitchen chair and stared blankly at the table. "Did you go to work today?"

Mary laughed. "Yes. Mark came by after work and we're having dinner."

"Did you spend the weekend with him?"

"I might have."

"Wow." Julie was silent for a moment.

Mary cleared her throat and when she spoke, her voice was hushed. "I kinda like him, Jules. He's funny and good looking, and he's got a steady job. When was the last time I met someone who had a goddamn job?"

"Good for you, Mary." Julie could feel her stomach turning. Things always worked out for Mary and she tried not to let her bitterness show. She really was happy for Mary but it only reminded her of her own loss.

"Jules? Is there something wrong?"

"No. I just wanted to hear your voice," she sighed.

"How did it go with Court?" Mary asked quietly.

"Fine. He uh, he spent the weekend with me. He gave me his cell phone but I don't think I'm going to call him again. What's the point, you know? We can't have a relationship."

"Oh, Jules," Mary said. "I'll be right over."

"No! Don't, Mary. I'm fine, honestly. Enjoy your dinner with Mark and you can come over tomorrow night and we'll talk, okay?"

Mary hesitated. "Jules, listen to me. There's something strange about Court."

"What do you mean?"

"Well, Mark's his best friend and he hasn't said a word to me about Court being a, you know, escort. I mean, he talks about working with him in construction but that's it. Did you know that Court owns his own construction company?"

"I – well, I knew he worked in construction," Julie stuttered. "I didn't know he owned his own company."

"Well, he does. Why would a man who owns his own company be working as an escort? And from what I can tell he's never spoken a word to Mark about it."

"Why would he? I doubt he wants many people to know," Julie replied. She stood up and moved into the living room, staring sightlessly out the large bay window.

"Yeah, I guess. Still, something doesn't seem right. Promise me you won't call him or see him until we find out more about him, okay?"

Lights flashed in her driveway and she squinted at the strange car that had pulled in. Her heart skipped a beat when Court unfolded his long legs from the car and walked quickly toward her front door.

"Julie? Do you hear me?"

"Yeah. I need to go, Mary. I'll call you tomorrow." She hung up before Mary could reply and hurried to the front door. She pulled it open before Court could knock, unable to stop the smile from crossing her face.

"Hi!"

"Hi, Julie." Court gave her a nervous smile. "Can I come in?"

"Of course." She glanced at the car. "Where's your truck?"

"Oh, uh, it's at the garage. This is a rental." He stood nervously in the hallway and she gave him a tentative smile.

"Are you all right?"

"Yes. Well, not really. Can we talk?"

"Sure. Come in the kitchen."

He followed her down the hallway and sat down at the table.

"Would you like some tea? Or a beer? I think there might be one or two in the back of the fridge."

He shook his head. "No, thanks."

She sat down and studied him carefully. There was something off about him, a jittery nervousness that he couldn't hide, and she gave him a curious look.

"What's wrong, Court?"

"I – " he hesitated and then plunged forward, "I'm in trouble, Julie. I owe some money to some pretty bad people and if I don't pay them by the end of this week...."

He trailed off and raked his hand through his hair. "I hate to ask you this but I wondered if I could borrow the cash from you. I'll pay you back, I swear."

She stared quietly at him for a moment. "Is this why you work as an escort when you own your own company?"

"What?" He stared blankly at her before nodding. "Yeah, that's the reason."

He gave her a pleading look. "What do you say, Julie? Could you help me out? I'm desperate here."

She nodded. "Of course I will. How much do you need?"

He took a deep breath. "Fifty thousand."

"I can get you the money by tomorrow. Does that work for you?"

"Yeah, it does. Thanks, Julie. I swear to God I'll pay you back."

"I know." She smiled at him and he reached out and took her hand, squeezing it lightly.

"You're the best, Julie. I can't tell you how much I – "

He stopped. Julie's face had paled and she was staring at his hands.

"What's wrong?"

"Your hands," she whispered.

He blinked and stared at his hands. They looked normal to him but she yanked her hands away and stood up when he tried to take her hand again.

"Julie? Honey, everything's fine. There's nothing wrong with my hands."

She barked harsh laughter. "I don't know who you are but I want you to get the hell out of my house. Do you hear me?"

She backed out of the kitchen as he stood and followed her down the hallway. "Julie, just relax. It's me, Court."

"No, you're not." There was a heavy statue on a side table in the hallway and she picked it up, holding it like a weapon as she reached for the door handle. "I want you to leave. Now."

She opened the door and shrieked with surprise when she heard Court's deep voice.

"Jules? What's going on?"

She turned, her face paling as the statue fell from her hand and landed with a thud on the floor. She stared wide-eyed at him before turning to look behind her. Court followed her gaze. Cal gave him a nervous look.

"Hey, Court."

"What the fuck?" Julie whispered. She pressed up against the wall and stared at the two of them.

"What the hell are you doing here, Cal?" Court ground out.

"Court, listen to me. I'm in trouble, okay? That investment thing, it wasn't what I said it was. I gave a bunch of money to this guy who – who said he had a sure deal. I was going to make back my money and then some. Only, the deal went wrong and he lost it all. I borrowed the money from Jimmy Golden and he wants it back."

"Jimmy Golden? You borrowed the money from a goddamn crime lord?" Court's voice was rising and Julie cringed back against the wall.

"He's not a crime lord. He's just a businessman," Cal said defensively.

"A businessman who breaks his client's legs when they don't pay up! Jesus, Cal! What were you thinking?" Court shouted.

Julie made a soft, whispering moan and closed her eyes. Court touched her arm gently and she flinched and pulled away from him. "Don't touch me."

"I'm sorry, darlin'. I can explain everything," he said pleadingly.

"Can you?" The look of betrayal in her eyes made his stomach turn.

"I can. I promise you. This is Cal, my twin brother."

"Yeah, I figured that part out," she whispered.

"Cal needed my help. He's the escort but he couldn't make your initial appointment so I pretended to be him. Only, I really liked you, Jules and so when you called again, I made Cal let me take his place."

"You lied to me," she whispered.

"I was going to tell you the truth. I swear it. That's why I'm here."

"I paid you to have sex with me and you're not – not even an escort?" She swallowed thickly.

"I never took the money," he said softly. "It went to Cal."

She studied Cal for a moment before turning back to Court. "Why? Why would you do this? I trusted you, Court. Did you and your brother have some – some sort of plan to con the lonely, rich spinster out of her money?"

"What? No! I swear, Julie! I had no idea that Cal was in trouble. I'm so sorry, Jules. I just, I didn't know how to tell you, and you were so sweet and you made me want you so badly that I – "

"So this is my fault?" She glared at him. "Is that what you're saying?"

"No! Darlin', just give me a minute with my brother and then we'll talk. I'll make you understand why I – "

"No. Get out, Court. Both of you get out, right now."

"Jules, please. Let me explain."

"I want you to leave. Take your brother and go, or I swear I'll call the police."

Cal stepped forward. "Julie, you can't tell the agency about this. If they find out that I let Court take my place, they'll fire me and I need the money. I can't – "

"Shut up, Cal!" Court roared.

Julie cringed again and Court reached out to touch her. "Don't be afraid, Jules. I won't hurt you. Please, just let me – "

"Get out!" She suddenly shrieked at him. "Get out of my house right now!" She pounded on his chest as tears poured down her cheeks. "Do you hear me? Get out!"

Cal was suddenly standing beside him and he took Court's arm and yanked him out of the house.

"Let go of me, Cal!"

"Court, it's over. Walk away, man!" Cal shouted as Julie slammed the door in their faces.

Court, his body shaking with anger, punched Cal in the face. Cal fell to the ground and touched his face, staring with shock at the blood that was dripping out of his nose.

"You hit me."

"I'll never forgive you for this! Do you hear me, Cal? Stay away from me, you goddamn bastard!" Court shouted before turning and stalking over to his truck. He climbed in and tore out of the driveway, tires squealing, as Cal slowly staggered to his feet.

He stood in front of the door for a moment before leaning closer to it. "Julie?"

Julie bit her lip and rested her head against the door as Cal's voice came through the door.

"I'm sorry, Julie. For what it's worth – Court doesn't care about your money. He didn't want to take my place that first night. I begged him to because I would have lost my job if he didn't and well, I need the money."

He laughed bitterly. "Court's a good guy, Julie. He's a better man than I'll ever be and I swear to you that he never meant to hurt you. He – he cares about you. I've never seen him act this way over a woman before."

She stuffed her hand into her mouth to stifle the sobs as tears zig-zagged their way down her cheeks.

"He's worth forgiving. He really is," Cal said loudly. She heard him walk away and the faint sound of his car starting. She sank to the floor and buried her face in her hands as she sobbed bitterly.

Chapter 11

Julie opened the door and stared at the dark-haired woman standing on her doorstep.

"Can I help you?"

"Julie?"

"Yes." Julie gave her a wary look as the woman smiled and held out her hand.

"My name is Melanie. Melanie Thomas?"

Julie looked at her blankly as she shook her hand and the woman gave her an uncomfortable look. "I'm Court and Cal's sister."

Julie dropped her hand and took a step back. "What do you want?"

"I wondered if we could speak for a moment about Court?"

"Do you always fight your brother's battles?"

The woman flushed. "Court doesn't know I'm here. And would seriously kill me if he did."

Julie started to close the door. "I'm sorry. I'm not interested in speaking with you. Please go away."

"I know you gave Cal money," Melanie said hurriedly.

"I don't know what you're talking about," Julie replied.

Melanie sighed softly. "Please, Julie, can I come in just for a minute?"

Julie hesitated and then stepped back. "Hell, why not. Let's find out if you're as messed up as your brothers."

* * *

Melanie sipped at the steaming cup of tea before smiling at Julie. "Thanks. This is really good."

"You're welcome."

Julie crossed her legs and held her own cup of tea as Melanie stared thoughtfully at her. "I can see why my brother likes you. You're very pretty and sweet."

"You don't even know me."

Melanie nodded. "That's true. Although, now that Court refuses to talk to Cal, I've been spending a great deal of time with Cal. He's not much for keeping secrets. He told me everything that happened."

Julie flushed and stared into her cup of tea. "Oh great. This just gets better and better. Does your entire family know about me now? The thirty-year-old virgin who had to pay a man to deflower her."

"No. Cal only told me," Melanie replied.

Julie took a sip of tea and stared silently at her.

"Why did you give Cal the money?" Melanie asked quietly.

"I didn't."

"You did. I know you did," Melanie replied. "There is no one Cal knows who could afford to courier him a cashier's cheque for fifty grand."

Julie didn't reply and Melanie took another sip of her tea. "Cal wanted to come here and tell you thank you. I wouldn't let him because I didn't think it was a great idea, but you should know that he's beyond grateful to you. You saved his life, you know."

"I didn't do it for him," Julie said.

"I figured." Melanie smiled gently at her. "Cal doesn't exactly have a way with the ladies. He's charming enough and he knows all the right things to say but he was never great at relationships. It's why he's so good at being an escort."

She sighed heavily. "Court on the other hand, well, he's never been good at loving them and leaving them. He was in this relationship with this bitch of a woman for nearly two years. Did he tell you about her? She put him through the wringer but it wasn't until he caught her cheating on him that he finally kicked her out. He's not weak, don't get me wrong, he just – he sees the good in people, you know? Even the rotten ones. He believes that there's good in everyone."

Julie could feel the tears sliding down her cheeks. "Why are you here? Why are you telling me this?" She whispered.

"Because I love my brother and he is miserable without you," Melanie said. "And forgive me, but I think you're just as miserable without him."

"He lied to me." Julie swiped at her cheeks.

"Yeah, I didn't say he wasn't stupid. I just said he was miserable." Melanie rolled her eyes and Julie couldn't hold back the small smile.

Melanie returned her smile. "I want you to consider giving Court a second chance. I wasn't kidding when I said he was miserable without you. He hasn't been to work in the week since the shit hit the fan. Hell, he hasn't left his apartment. He refuses to speak to Cal and he won't even talk to my parents. Dad's threatening to kidnap him and take him to the mountains again."

Julie smiled again. "He told me about that."

"Did he?" Melanie grinned. "Yeah, dad likes to bring that story up at every family reunion. It's like his greatest parenting moment, ever."

She leaned forward and gave Julie a searching look. "Listen, I know what my brother did was absolutely, without a doubt, the stupidest thing he could ever do but I truly believe that he cares about you. And I know you care about him or you wouldn't have given Cal the money and saved his ass. You could have called the escort agency and gotten Cal fired but instead, you kept your mouth shut and sent him fifty thousand dollars. I know you didn't do that for Cal. He's charming but he's not that goddamn charming."

She finished drinking her tea and stood up. "I'd better go. I've taken up enough of your time. Just, please Julie, think about forgiving my brother and giving him a second chance. I swear he's worth it."

Julie nodded and followed Melanie to the front door. Melanie stepped outside and smiled at her. "It was nice to meet you, Julie."

"It was nice to meet you too," Julie replied.

She shut the door as Melanie turned and walked away, and leaned heavily against it. Her mind was whirling and her pulse was thudding in her ears. She yanked open the front door.

"Melanie?"

Melanie paused with her hand on her car door. "Yeah?"

"I've thought about it. Will you take me to your brother's apartment?"

Melanie, a huge grin crossing her face, nodded. "Yes, I can do that."

* * *

"Jesus, Court. Open a window in here, for the love of God." His sister's voice rang down the hallway and he sighed and turned up the volume on the TV.

"Go away, Mel. I don't want company."

"Yeah, that's apparent." His sister walked into the living room, her nose wrinkling with disgust.

"Did mom send you over here? Tell her I'm fine," Court snapped as she crossed the room and opened the blinds.

He blinked at the bright light. "I prefer the blinds closed."

Mel ignored him and shoved open the window. "Mom didn't send me. She's having dinner with dad and Cal."

"Cal? I would have figured he was in the hospital with two busted legs by now," Court said grouchily. He stared at the flickering light of the television as Mel snatched the remote from his hand and muted it.

"You know Cal. He always bounces back."

"Yeah," Court replied bitterly. He glanced at his sister. "Can you go? I'm tired. I want to go to bed."

"It's only five-thirty, you big dumb lug. Besides, you've got company."

"What?" He blinked at her as she pointed behind him.

"I said you've got company."

He twisted around, his mouth dropping open as he stared at Julie standing in the doorway of the living room.

"What — what are you doing here?" He rasped. He stood up from the couch, acutely aware of the stained t-shirt and shorts he was wearing and the scraggly beard he was sporting.

"I thought we should talk," she whispered.

"Well, I'm gonna go," Mel said cheerfully. "Call me later, big brother."

She squeezed Julie's shoulder as she slipped by, and he took a nervous step toward Julie as he heard the front door shut.

"You look good," he whispered.

"Thanks. You look um…"

She stared at him and he grimaced.

"Yeah, I know what I look like. How have you been?"

She shrugged. "Okay. Better than I was."

"I'm so sorry, Julie," he said hoarsely. "I never meant to hurt you. I swear I didn't. It was stupid of me to lie and I wish to God I hadn't."

"I know," she said simply. "I forgive you for lying to me."

"You do?" He was standing in front of her now and he wanted to reach out and touch her but he kept his hands closed into fists at his sides.

"Yes." She didn't say anything else, just regarded him solemnly and he closed his eyes.

"I've missed you," he whispered.

For a moment there was nothing and he could feel despair washing over him. She might have forgiven him but she would never take him back. She would never let him –

"I've missed you too." Her soft hands were cupping his face and he opened his eyes to see her face only inches from his. "It's ridiculous how much I've missed you," she said before she pressed her mouth against his.

He groaned and wrapped his arms around her waist, yanking her into his embrace as he kissed her warm mouth repeatedly.

"I'm sorry, I'm so sorry," he whispered.

"Stop. Don't apologize anymore, okay?" She rested her forehead against his and he stroked her back through her t-shirt.

"You're so beautiful," he whispered. "You smell so good." He buried his face in her throat and inhaled deeply.

"Thank you." She tugged at his hair until he raised his head. "You smell terrible."

He burst out laughing and she grinned before wrinkling her nose. "I mean, really, really terrible."

"I haven't showered in a few days," he admitted.

"I can tell." She stepped out of his embrace and took his hand. "Where's your bathroom."

"Down the hall."

He followed her into the washroom and watched as she turned on the shower, testing the water with her hand before she pulled his t-shirt over his head. She studied him in the bright light of the bathroom.

"When was the last time you slept?"

He shrugged. "I don't know. A couple of days. I kept dreaming of you, and after a while I figured it would be easier just not to sleep."

She frowned at him. "Court, that's a really stupid thing to do."

He didn't reply. He was running his hands over her arms as if he thought she would disappear and she tugged on his shorts. "Get in the shower, Court."

"Will you join me?"

She shook her head. "I'd better not. You need to get some sleep and if I climb into the shower with you, you won't get any. We both know that."

"I don't need sleep. I need you." He reached for her and she stepped back.

"What you need is to brush your teeth, shave and have a shower," she said pointedly. "I'll wait for you in your bedroom."

* * *

When he walked into his bedroom, she was lying in his bed. He nearly ran across the room and crawled into the bed, pressing himself eagerly against her warm, naked curves.

She put her arm around him and pulled him close. "You smell much better."

He smiled and nuzzled her neck. "I feel better."

"Good." She stroked his chest. "You should get some sleep, Court."

"I'm not tired." He was aching for her, his cock hard as a rock, but he made himself stroke her side instead of cupping her breast the way he wanted to.

She slipped her hand under the covers and grasped his cock, making him moan with need. "I can tell."

"Please, Jules. I need you," he whispered.

"I need you too," she murmured. She slipped on top of him and rubbed herself against his cock before leaning over him and kissing him deeply.

He returned her kiss eagerly, pushing his tongue into her mouth as he cupped and kneaded her breasts.

She pulled back and showed him the condom in her hand. "I found this in your bedside table."

She ripped it open and shifted backwards until she was straddling his thighs. She rolled it on carefully, biting her lip in concentration, and he nearly came in her hand when she stroked him lightly.

"I can't wait, darlin'," he moaned.

"Me either." She held his cock in one hand and lowered herself on to him. He blew his breath out in a harsh rush as she rode him with slow, careful strokes.

"Christ, that feels so fucking good," he moaned.

"Touch me, Court. Make me come," she demanded.

He moved his hand to her clit and rubbed it as she moved faster. She slid up and down his throbbing cock as he rubbed furiously at her clit. She moaned and gasped with pleasure and he gave a hoarse shout of surprise when she suddenly came with a short cry.

"Julie!" He gasped her name as her pussy squeezed around him and he was helpless to stop from coming.

She stared down at him as he panted beneath her and he reddened slightly. "Sorry, darlin'."

"For what?" She asked curiously.

"I usually have better control," he muttered.

"I like making you lose control."

She slid off of him and he pulled off the condom and disposed of it before pulling her into his arms. She rested her head against his chest and sighed happily.

He stroked her warm back. "How did you know Cal wasn't me? When I went to your house that night I heard you yelling at him. How did you know?"

She took his hand and rubbed her fingers across the calluses on his palm before linking their fingers together. "Your hands."

"My hands?"

"Cal took my hand and his was smooth." She smiled up at him. "No calluses."

"How did you meet my sister?" He gave her a curious look.

"She came to my house and asked me to give you a second chance."

He groaned loudly. "Christ, that's embarrassing."

She shrugged. "Your sister loves you and so does your brother."

He scowled at the mention of his brother and she rubbed her hand over his chest. "I need to tell you something, Court."

"What?" He kissed her forehead as she took a deep breath.

"I gave Cal the fifty thousand dollars."

His mouth dropped open. "You did what?"

"I gave him the money he needed."

"Jules, I – you shouldn't have done that. He'll never pay you back," he said quietly.

"I don't care about that," she replied.

"Why did you give him the money?"

"Because he's your brother and he was in trouble. Besides, as Mary says, I'm a rich bitch who'll never be able to spend all of my money anyway." She grinned at him. "Why not give it away?"

He gave her a troubled look. "Jules, I'll pay you back the money. It'll take me a little while but I promise – "

She put her hand over his mouth and gave him a stern look. "Oh no you will not, Court. This was a gift."

"It's a hell of a gift."

"I'm a hell of a woman?" She raised her eyebrows at him and he laughed.

"That you are, Julie Winslow." He kissed her forehead again. "Thank you for helping him, darlin'. He drives me crazy but I love him."

"I know you do and you need to forgive him for his part in all of this. Okay? People do crazy things when they're desperate."

"I know," he sighed. "I'll talk to him tomorrow."

"Good." She gave him a cat-like grin of satisfaction and he sighed and pulled her closer.

128

"I really am sorry for lying, Jules."

"I know. Go to sleep now," she said softly.

"Will you give me a second chance?" He whispered. "Will you – can we get to know each other again? Maybe go out for dinner or to a movie?"

She smiled in the dim light. "Are you asking me out on a date, Court?"

"I am." He held his breath.

"I'd love to go on a date with you." She kissed his neck and he pressed his body against her warm one.

"I'll never hurt you again, Jules. I promise," he whispered.

"I know." She kissed him lightly on the lips before taking a deep breath. "I think I might be falling in love with you."

He grinned delightedly at her. "Well, that's a real shame because I *know* I'm falling in love with you."

"People don't just fall in love in four days. We must be crazy. You know that, right?"

He nodded. "Yep. And I've never been happier."

"Me either," she whispered. "I love you, Court."

"I love you too, Jules."

END

Please enjoy a sample chapter of Ramona Gray's novel, "Saving Jax".
Saving Jax tells the story of Court and Cal's youngest sister, Melanie.

Saving Jax

Copyright 2015 Ramona Gray

* * * *

"I have to admit, Mr. Thomas, I didn't believe you'd have my money."

"I told you I was good for it, Mr. Golden," Cal replied.

"So you did. But fifty thousand is a lot of money." Jimmy Golden smiled at him.

Cal didn't reply and Jimmy gave him a thoughtful look. "You're a good looking guy. Isn't he good looking, Jax?"

"Yes, sir."

Cal's eyes flickered to the man standing just to the left of Jimmy. He was shorter than Cal but he was at least six feet and his scarred face and dark suit made him appear dangerous.

"This is Jax Anderson. He works for me." Jimmy waved his hand in the general direction of Jax and Cal nodded to the man.

"Do you have any restaurant experience, Mr. Thomas?"

Cal blinked in surprise at the odd question. "I'm sorry?"

"Restaurant experience. Do you have any? Most young men have worked in the service industry at some point or the other. Did you?"

Cal shook his head. "No."

Jimmy leaned back in his chair and stroked the swell of his belly absentmindedly. "Do you enjoy being an escort, Mr. Thomas?"

Cal shrugged. "It pays the bills."

"Of which you have many."

Cal reddened. "How do you know that?"

"I know everything about you, Calvin Thomas," Jimmy said. He leaned forward and opened a brown file folder sitting on his gleaming desk. He perused it carefully. "You're thirty-three years old, you live in a rather dismal apartment in the west end, your parents are Darla and Bill Thomas, both retired. You have a twin brother named Courtney and a younger sister Melanie. You also owe thousands in personal credit card debt, a car loan and a personal loan. You're terrible with your finances."

Cal gritted his teeth and gave Jimmy a strained smile. "There are reasons for my debt that have nothing to do with poor financial choices."

"I'm sure," Jimmy said absently. "What do your parents think of your career choice? Are they ashamed that their son is paid to have sex with women?"

"They don't know," Cal said shortly.

"Interesting. What do they think you do for a living?" Jimmy steepled his fingers under his chin.

"They think I'm a limo driver."

Jimmy snorted. "Very clever. I suppose it explains the odd hours and late nights."

"It does." Cal glanced at his watch. "I don't mean to be rude, Mr. Golden, but I have another appointment to go to."

"Of course. So many lonely women, so little time," Jimmy replied.

Cal gave him a tight smile and started to rise.

"I'd like to offer you a job, Mr. Thomas."

Cal froze and then sank back into his chair. "I'm sorry?"

"I'm looking for someone to manage my restaurant. Well, it's more of a restaurant/night club, really. My manager recently relocated and I'd like you to take his place."

"That's very generous of you, Mr. Golden, but I'm afraid I'm not qualified for the job. I have no restaurant experience, remember?"

Jimmy shrugged. "Let me be honest with you, Mr. Thomas. What I'm really looking for is a young, good looking man to deal with my customers. I'm looking to grow my restaurant business and customer service is everything. If I have you there, greeting the customers and attending to their every need, I believe it would be beneficial."

He stared thoughtfully at Cal. "As an escort, you've already proven that you're excellent with people. You're accustomed to providing top-notch service, and you're good-looking and well-spoken. Do a good job and you'll be rewarded appropriately. I believe in allowing my employees to rise up in the ranks, so to speak."

He glanced behind him. "Jax here, started out as an errand boy for me. Didn't you, Jax?"

"Yes, sir."

"So, what do you say, Mr. Thomas? It won't pay as much as your escort work – at least, not at first – but it'll be a steady job, no waiting for a woman to pick your face from a website, and one that you can tell your parents about." A small smile crossed Jimmy's face.

Cal cleared his throat. "I appreciate the job offer, Mr. Golden. Could I have some time to think on it?"

"Of course." Jimmy sat forward and closed the file folder in front of him. "Have a good day, Mr. Thomas. We'll be in touch."

* * *

One week later.

"Hold on, I'm coming," Cal shouted as there was a second knock on the door. He dodged past the pile of boxes he'd never gotten around to unpacking and swung open the door. He blinked in surprise at the man standing in the doorway.

"Good evening, Mr. Thomas."

"Hey. Jax, right?"

"Yes. May I come in?"

"Sure." Cal led Jax down the crowded hallway to the small kitchen. "Can I get you a coffee? Beer?"

"No thank you." Jax stared at the dishes piled in the sink and the laundry and flyers on the small wooden table.

"Sorry about the mess." Cal cleared a spot on one of the chairs and Jax unbuttoned his suit jacket and sat down.

"Mr. Golden would like to know if you're accepting his job offer."

Cal sat down and took a drink of beer. "He didn't come himself?"

"Mr. Golden is a very busy man," Jax replied.

Cal drummed his fingers on the top of the table. "What exactly do you do for Mr. Golden?"

Jax straightened the sleeves of his jacket before folding his hands in his lap. "Personal protection."

Cal raised his eyebrows. "What would Mr. Golden need protection from?"

He knew the rumours as well as everyone else. Jimmy Golden might have appeared to be nothing more than a successful entrepreneur but there were suggestions that he was involved with smuggling and dealing drugs in large quantities.

Jax shrugged. "A man in Mr. Golden's position can have many enemies."

"Do you enjoy working for him?"

"I do. Mr. Golden can be a very generous man to his employees."

Cal ran a hand through his short hair. "I'll be honest, Jax. I don't understand why Mr. Golden is offering this job to me. I have zero experience."

Jax crossed one leg over the other and leaned back in the chair. "Mr. Golden has the ability to see potential in people. He believes in your abilities to do the job."

When Cal didn't reply, he sighed lightly. "This is a fantastic opportunity for you, Cal. Do an excellent job, show your loyalty to Mr. Golden, and he'll give you the chance to do very well for yourself."

"How did you start working for him?" Cal asked curiously. His eyes travelled over the thin scar that ran from Jax's temple to the middle of his throat.

"I was a troubled kid and teenager. At the time, Mr. Golden owned a chain of convenience stores. I was caught stealing from one of them. I was brought to Mr. Golden and he saw my potential and offered me a job working for him. I could accept the job or be arrested. Naturally, I accepted the job."

"No regrets?" Cal asked curiously.

Jax hesitated and a strange look flickered across his face for a brief moment. "No regrets."

"Are you sure about that?"

"Yes," Jax said impatiently. "Listen, all you need to remember is that Mr. Golden values loyalty above all else. Do a good job, show your loyalty, and there won't be a problem."

"And if I don't?" Cal asked.

"Then Mr. Golden will have me break your kneecaps," Jax replied calmly.

Cal's mouth dropped open and he stared silently at the man. He jerked in surprise when Jax suddenly grinned at him, revealing even white teeth. "Just kidding."

Cal shook his head and snorted lightly. "Nice."

"Are you taking the job, Mr. Thomas?"

Cal rubbed at his forehead for a moment. He had spent a great deal of time mulling over Mr. Golden's job offer. With Court refusing to talk to him and an uncharacteristically slow time at the escort agency, he'd had plenty of time to consider it.

He took a deep breath and nodded. "Yes. Tell Mr. Golden I'll take the job."

"Excellent, Mr. Thomas." Jax grinned again at him.

"Call me Cal."

Jax stood. "Mr. Golden would like you to start Monday. Be at the restaurant at four," he pulled a card from his pocket, "and wear a nice suit. This is the address for the restaurant." He took a pen from the inside pocket of his suit jacket and jotted down a phone number on the back of it. "This is my cell number. You can call me anytime if you have – "

"Cal, it worked!"

His front door slammed shut and his sister's voice drifted down the hall. She wandered into the kitchen, pulling off her jacket. "I got Court and Julie back together."

Cal stared at her. "You're kidding me!"

She grinned smugly at him. "Nope! I just finished dropping Julie off at Court's place, and I wouldn't be surprised if they're having sex right this very min – "

She broke off and turned a soft shade of pink as she noticed the man standing in Cal's kitchen.

Cal cleared his throat. "Mel, this is Jax Anderson. Jax, this is my sister, Melanie Thomas."

Melanie gave the man standing in front of her a quick once over. He was tall and lean with dark hair and bright blue eyes. His dark suit fit him perfectly, she suspected it was tailored, and there was a hardness to him that made her nervous. The scar running from his temple to his throat, didn't help.

"It's a pleasure to meet you, Ms. Thomas."

She realized with embarrassment that Jax was holding out his hand and she took a step toward him and took his hand. His voice, deep and raspy, was doing weird things to her insides and when his hard hand swallowed hers in a tight grip, she felt a tingle of lust sweep through her.

What the hell?

"Nice to meet you as well, Mr. Anderson."

She gave him a faint smile and tried to drop his hand. He held it for a moment longer and she wasn't sure what was heating her up more, the touch of his hand or the look in his eyes. He released her hand and the spell was broken. She took a deep breath and stared at the floor as Jax turned to Cal.

"Call me if you have any questions, Cal. Otherwise, we'll see you on Monday."

"Thanks, Jax." Cal walked him to the front door and Melanie collapsed in one of the kitchen chairs. She was trembling and there were butterflies in her stomach, and she took a shaky breath.

Get it together, Thomas. He's just a man.

"Who was that?" She asked, the moment Cal returned to the kitchen.

"I told you, Jax Anderson."

She rolled her eyes. "Does he, uh, work at the agency with you?"

Cal snorted. "God, no."

She hadn't thought so. She didn't think there was a woman alive who would take one look at him and purposely decide she wanted him in her bed. He was handsome enough, downright fucking gorgeous in fact, but there was something about him that practically screamed danger.

He was the kind of man who would look perfectly at ease with a gun in his hand. The kind of man who had rough sex with a barely-willing woman and didn't think twice about it. The kind of man who –

"Are Court and Julie really back together?" Cal's voice interrupted her thoughts.

She nodded. "Yeah, I think so. I talked with Julie and she asked me to take her to Court's. They looked like they were going to kiss and make up."

"Thank God," Cal muttered as Mel opened the fridge and grabbed a bottle of water.

She surveyed the nearly-empty fridge. "Do you have any money for food, Cal?"

"I'm fine," he snapped. "Did you tell Julie I said thank you?"

Mel nodded and dropped into the chair across from his. She took a drink of water and eyed him thoughtfully. "Who was that guy?"

"I already told you, Jax Anderson."

She snorted in frustration and took another swig of water. "Why are you avoiding the question?"

"I'm not."

"You are."

Cal cracked his knuckles nervously. "Fine. When I paid Mr. Golden back the money I owed him, he offered me a job."

Mel set her water bottle down with a thump. "Tell me you didn't take the job, Cal."

"You don't even know what it is."

"I know that Golden's a – a friggin' mob boss and you don't need to be involved with him!" She nearly shouted.

He rolled his eyes. "He's not a mob boss, Mel. Jesus, where do you come up with this shit? Just because a guy is a successful business owner doesn't make him the head of the mob."

"Don't start with me, Cal. You've heard the rumours like I have. Besides, the guy would have broken your legs if Julie hadn't saved your ass and given you the fifty grand you owed him, and you know it. You couldn't possibly think working for a guy like him is a smart move."

"I took the job."

"You what?" This time she did shout and Cal winced before holding his hands up.

"Calm down, Mel! Christ, do you want the neighbours to call the cops?"

"Cal, you can't work for this man. Listen, I know you're desperate for money but – "

"It's not just about the money!" He interrupted her with a sharp bang of his fist on the table. "Did you ever think that maybe, just maybe, I'm tired of being an escort? I know you and Court think it's a big joke that I fuck women for money but it isn't, okay? Do you know what it's like to have to fuck a different woman nearly every night? I know I'm not great at relationships but even I get tired of sleeping around. And I'm tired of lying to mom and dad about what I do. I worry every day that they'll find out and if they think I'm a disappointment now, what will they think when they find out I'm a damn escort?"

He stopped, breathing heavily and glaring angrily at her, and she reached out and squeezed his fist. "You're not a disappointment to mom and dad, Cal."

"Yeah," he muttered before looking down at the table.

She sighed softly and squeezed his hand again. "What will you be doing for Golden?"

"I'll be managing his restaurant."

She blinked in surprise. "Really? You don't have any restaurant experience."

"I told him that but he has faith in me. Is that so hard to believe?" There was a note of bitterness in his voice and she shook her head quickly.

"No, of course not. I just – I would have thought he'd look for someone with experience, that's all."

"Jax says Mr. Golden likes to give people chances. To give them the opportunity to work their way up. I'm just managing right now but who knows where I could be in ten years. Working for Mr. Golden could open up a lot of doors for me."

"So this Jax guy works for Golden?" She asked.

He nodded. "Yeah. Personal security."

"Surprise, surprise," she muttered.

He frowned. "What's that supposed to mean?"

"The man looks dangerous." She arched her eyebrow at him. "How did he get that scar on his face?"

Cal shrugged. "I didn't ask. I hardly know the guy."

"Cal?" Melanie gave him a hesitant look. "Are you sure you know what you're doing?"

"Yes," he said firmly. "This is a good thing, Mel."

He glanced at his cell phone. "Listen, I need to call Vanessa and tell her I'm quitting. Do you mind?"

She shook her head and stood up before giving him a quick kiss on the forehead. "Are you coming to dinner on Thursday night? Mom's expecting all of us."

He nodded. "Yeah, unless I'm working that night."

He caught her hand as she turned to leave. "Hey, do you really think Court and Julie are back together?"

She nodded. "Pretty sure."

"Good. He deserves someone better than that bitch Janine."

"Yeah, he does. Hopefully Julie's not like her."

"I don't think she is." He walked her to the door. "I'll talk to you later, Mel."

"Bye, honey." She kissed his cheek and frowned when he ruffled her long, dark hair.

"Stop it, butthead."

"Whatever, gator breath."

She stuck her tongue out at him and left.

Please enjoy a sample chapter of Ramona Gray's newest novella: "The Vampire's Kiss".

* * * *

THE VAMPIRE'S KISS

(Other World Series Book One)

Copyright 2014 Ramona Gray

Abigail Winters had no idea what was happening. One minute she had been hurrying home from her mundane job as a coffee barista in the worse thunderstorm she had ever seen. The next, she was lying flat on her back in the middle of a forest with the rain falling on her face.

She sat up, rubbing the knot that was forming on the back of her head, and peered around curiously. She was sure she had seen a bright orb of light hovering to the left of her before everything went black. She looked around for her purse, wanting to grab her cell phone and call someone. Who she wasn't sure – the police maybe.

Her purse was nowhere to be seen and she sighed and stood cautiously, waiting to see if she was going to pass out. Her head was aching and her new jeans, the ones she had been so proud to buy because they were a size smaller than her last pair, were shredded at the knees and covered in mud.

Was she dead? Didn't people say that there was a white light when you died? She looked around as the rain continued to fall. It was dark and scary and if this was heaven, she would hate to see what hell looked like.

She moved forward slowly, squinting in the dark and watching her feet so she didn't trip over the exposed roots of the trees around her.

She was frightened, but not panicking. At least, not yet. There was a part of her, a very large part, which was convinced she was dreaming. Any moment now she would wake up in her bed with the sheets tangled around her legs and her alarm clock shrieking at her.

She took a deep breath. The air smelled sweet and clean, nothing like the smog of the city, and she wondered vaguely if someone had kidnapped her and dumped her in the country.

Don't be ridiculous, Abby. Who would kidnap you? You're a nobody.

All perfectly true. She wasn't an heiress with a million-dollar inheritance, she wasn't a famous singer or movie star. Truth be told she had less than twenty dollars in her bank account at the moment. She was just plain, fat Abby. Always had been, always would be.

Yes, but don't forget that you're fat Abby with fifteen pounds less fat.

Also true. She ran her hands down her size eighteen jeans. She had been thrilled when she had gone down a size in pants. She carried most of her weight in her ass and her hips, and to be down a pants size meant that her healthy eating and exercising was working. She hated exercising but she was becoming addicted to the results.

Um, Abby? Not to rain on your parade but in case you've forgotten, you're either dead or something very, very weird is going on. Maybe celebrate your weight loss victory another time, what do you say?

Very good advice. If she wasn't dead then she needed to find the nearest phone and call the police.

She stumbled through the trees. She had no idea if she was moving deeper into the woods or not but she couldn't just stand there. She had to keep moving.

"She looks like a lost lamb. Does she not, Toron?"

Abby shrieked and whipped around. Two men were standing behind her. They were dressed similarly in faded green pants and white shirts. One was tall and dark and the other short and blond.

"Aye, she does, Alex," the blond man said gravely.

"Are you lost little lamb? Lost in the woods?" The one named Toron crooned softly.

Abby backed up a step. There was something about the two men that was making all the hair on her body attempt to stand up. Adrenaline was flooding through her veins and her limbs trembled in response.

She stumbled back another step as the men moved closer. Alex inhaled deeply. "I can smell her fear. It smells delicious."

Toron grinned at him. "I'm feeling generous this evening. Why don't you have the first drink?"

"Don't mind if I do," Alex said cheerfully. He was standing in front of her and pushing her against a tree before Abby had realized he'd moved.

Her head banged on the tree, the knot screaming in protest, and she screamed shrilly into the cold night air.

"Oh yes, little lamb – go ahead and scream. There's no one to hear you and I do love it when the lambs scream," Alex whispered.

He was holding her with one hand across the top of her chest and she grabbed his arm and tried to yank it away from her. His arm was hard as iron. She struggled futilely, unable to believe that the small man could hold her so easily with just one hand. She stared at his pale skin, her eyes dark and wide with panic, and he giggled like a demented child.

"You're a big one but I don't mind. More of you to drink, right?"

She slapped him across the face as hard as she could. His head rocked back but his hand never moved from her chest.

He hissed at her and she screamed as fresh adrenaline poured into her veins. Alex was grinning at her and exposing his long, white fangs.

"You don't ever want to hit me, little lamb. Not that it matters – you'll be dead in a few minutes."

"Oh get on with it, would you, Alex. I want my turn. You shouldn't play with your food anyway. Didn't your mother ever tell – "

Toron suddenly arched his back as a startled look crossed his face. "Alex – "

Abby sucked in her breath when Toron suddenly exploded in a shower of ash and blood. Alex screamed, a sound of rage and fear, at the man standing in the trees. He held a long, curved blade in one hand and he smiled bitterly at Alex.

"You would kill your own kind!" Alex screamed again and, forgetting Abby entirely, he lunged for the stranger. His fingernails were lengthening, becoming long and wickedly sharp talons, and he moved so quickly that he was nothing but a blur.

Alex was quick but the stranger was faster. The blade plunged through Alex's chest and his scream of fury became a long, gurgling moan. Abby sunk to the ground, wrapping her arms around her knees as the stranger yanked the blade free and wiped it on Alex's shirt. He stepped back just as Alex exploded.

Abby watched disinterestedly as the man approached her, sheathing his blade into the holder at his waist. He crouched in front of her and took her chin in his hand, tilting her head first one way and then the other as he examined her neck.

He was tall and broad with long dark hair tied back in a neat ponytail. His eyes were a silvery grey and his skin was pale and smooth. He had a broad nose and high cheekbones, and his jaw was covered in dark stubble.

"Are you going to kill me?" Abby asked dully.

He shook his head. "No. Get up, girl."

He heaved her to her feet with one hard hand under her arm and gave her a look of disgust when she swayed. He eyed her up and down and another grimace of disgust passed across his face.

She would have been offended if she hadn't noticed his teeth. They were very white and, despite the rain and the darkness, she had no problem seeing his fangs. She moaned softly and he shook his head impatiently.

"I said I wouldn't hurt you. Come on, girl." He dragged her through the trees, moving so quickly that she was soon out of breath and struggling to catch up.

He grunted with frustration and slowed down a fraction, his hand tightening on her wrist when she tried to pull free.

"Please let go of me," she panted.

"So you can run? You'll be dead before morning if I do," he snapped.

"Where are we going?"

"I'm taking you to your own kind. Now keep your mouth shut and hurry up."

In less than fifteen minutes they were at the edge of the forest. He stopped, his eyes roaming the large field in front of them. She stood next to him, panting and trying to control her runaway heartbeat as he rolled his eyes.

"Have you considered eating less and moving more, human?"

"Fuck you," she puffed.

He laughed. "The lamb shows spirit."

She glared at him and he suddenly cupped her face and pulled her forward until her face was only inches from his. He grinned at her, his fangs looking very long and very sharp, and she swallowed nervously.

"Although I do enjoy fucking a human, you're not my type." He let his gaze travel down her body and back up to her face. "A little too big for my tastes. Still, you are rather attractive – perhaps I could make an exception."

She flushed bright red and yanked her head from his grip. He returned his gaze to the field. "We're going to be moving very quickly across the field. Keep up. You'll regret it if you don't. Do you understand me?"

He stared into her dark brown eyes. His eyes were grey and cold and she nodded, although she was almost positive that she would not be able to keep up with him. She wasn't going to tell him that. He would probably kill her rather than give her the chance to try.

"Good. Let's – "

He stopped, his head cocked to the side, and his eyebrows drew down in a frown.

"What – "

"Shut up!" He hissed.

She closed her mouth with a snap as he dropped her wrist. She took a few steps backward, wondering if she could sneak away without him noticing. Before she could dart into the trees, a silver mesh dropped on to the man in front of her.

He hissed in agony as he collapsed to the ground. She watched in horror as his skin began to smoke. She reached for the net but two men and a woman dropped from the skies above her and blocked her from grabbing it.

"Hello human." The woman smiled at her, revealing her own set of fangs, and Abby moaned with terror.

Follow Ramona on Twitter or Facebook for updates and release date information.

If you would like more information about Ramona Gray, please visit her at:

www.ramonagray.ca

or

https://www.facebook.com/RamonaGrayBooks

or

https://twitter.com/RamonaGrayBooks

Books by Ramona Gray

The Vampire's Kiss (Other World Series Book One)
The Vampire's Love (Other World Series Book Two)
The Shifter's Mate (Other World Series Book Three)
Rescued by the Wolf (Other World Series Book Four)
The Escort
Saving Jax
The Assistant
One Night

Printed in Great Britain
by Amazon